TERROR ON THE ROAD

There was something to her right! Stevie saw something move, but she didn't know what it was.

"Stevie!" Carole cried.

"Look out!" Callie screamed from the backseat.

Stevie swerved to the left on the narrow road, hoping it would be enough. Her answer was a sickening jolt as the car slammed into something solid. The car spun around, smashing against the thing again. When the thing screamed, Stevie knew it was a horse. The car smashed against the guardrail on the left side of the road and tumbled up and over it as if the rail had never been there.

Down they went, rolling, spinning. Stevie could hear the screams of her friends. She could hear her own voice, echoing in the close confines of the car, answered by the thumps of the car rolling down the hillside into a gully. Suddenly the thumping stopped. The screams were stilled. The engine cut off. The wheels stopped spinning. And all Stevie could hear was the idle *slap, slap, slap* of her windshield wipers.

PINE HOLLOW™

THE LONG RIDE

BY BONNIE BRYANT

BANTAM BOOKS
NEW YORK • TORONTO • LONDON • SYDNEY • AUCKLAND

Special thanks to Sir "B" Farms and Laura and Vinny Marino

RL5.0, ages 12 and up

THE LONG RIDE
A Bantam Book / August 1998

"Pine Hollow" is a trademark of Bonnie Bryant Hiller.

ISBN 0-553-49242-X

Published simultaneously in the United States and Canada

Bantam Books are published by Bantam Books, a division of Bantam
Doubleday Dell Publishing Group, Inc. Its trademark, consisting of the
words "Bantam Books" and the portrayal of a rooster, is Registered in
U.S. Patent and Trademark Office and in other countries. Marca
Registrada. Bantam Books, 1540 Broadway, New York, New York 10036.

PRINTED IN THE UNITED STATES OF AMERICA

OPM   0 9 8 7 6 5 4 3 2 1

For my sister, Penny Carey

PROLOGUE

"Do you think we'll get there in time?" Stevie Lake asked, looking around for some sign that the airport was near.

"Since that plane almost landed on top of us, I think we're close," Carole Hanson said.

"Turn right here," said Callie Forester from the backseat.

"And then left up ahead," Carole advised, picking out directions from the signs that flashed past near the airport entrance. "I think Lisa's plane is leaving from that terminal there."

"Which one?"

"The one we just passed," Callie said.

"Oh," said Stevie. She gripped the steering wheel tightly and looked for a way to turn around without causing a major traffic tie-up.

"This would be easier if we were on horseback," said Carole.

"Everything's easier on horseback," Stevie agreed.

"Or if we had a police escort," said Callie.

"Have you done that?" Stevie asked, trying to maneuver the car across three lanes of traffic.

"Yeah," said Callie. "It's kind of fun, but dangerous. It makes you think you're almost as important as other people tell you you are."

Stevie rolled her window down and waved wildly at the confused drivers around her. Clearly, her waving confused them more, but it worked. All traffic stopped. She crossed the three lanes and pulled onto the service road.

It took another ten minutes to get back to the right and then ten more to find a parking place. Five minutes into the terminal. And then all that was left was to find Lisa.

"Where do you think she is?" Carole asked.

"I know," said Stevie. "Follow me."

"That's what we've been doing all morning," Callie said dryly. "And look how far it's gotten us."

But she followed anyway.

Alex Lake reached across the table in the airport cafeteria and took Lisa Atwood's hand.

"It's going to be a long summer," he said.

Lisa nodded. Saying good-bye was one of her least favorite activities. She didn't want Alex to know how hard it was, though. That would just make it tougher on him. The two of them had known each other for four years—as long as Lisa had been best friends with Alex's twin sister, Stevie. But they'd only started dating six months earlier. Lisa could hardly believe that. It seemed as if she'd been in love with him forever.

"But it is just for the summer," she said. The

2

words sounded dumb even as they came out of her mouth. The summer *was* long. She wouldn't come back to Virginia until right before school started.

"I wish your dad didn't live so far away, and I wish the summer weren't so long."

"It'll go fast," said Lisa.

"For you, maybe. You'll be in California, surfing or something. I'll just be here, mowing lawns."

"I've never surfed in my life—"

"Until now," said Alex. It was almost a challenge, and Lisa didn't like it.

"I don't want to fight with you," said Lisa.

"I don't want to fight with you, either," he said, relenting. "I'm sorry. It's just that I want things to be different. Not very different. Just a little different."

"Me too," said Lisa. She squeezed his hand. It was a way to keep from saying anything else, because she was afraid that if she tried to speak she might cry, and she hated it when she cried. It made her face red and puffy, but most of all, it told other people how she was feeling. She'd found it useful to keep her feelings to herself these days. Like Alex, she wanted things to be different, but she wanted them to be very different, not just a little. She sighed. That was slightly better than crying.

"I told you so," said Stevie to Callie and Carole.

Stevie had threaded her way through the airport terminal, straight to the cafeteria near the security checkpoint. And there, sitting next to the door, were her twin brother and her best friend.

"Surprise!" the three girls cried, crowding around the table.

"We just couldn't let you be the only one to say good-bye to Lisa," Carole said, sliding into the booth next to Alex.

"We had to be here, too. You understand that, don't you?" Stevie asked Lisa as she sat down next to her.

"You guys!" said Lisa, her face lighting up with joy. "I'm so glad you're here. I was afraid I wasn't going to see you for months and months!"

She *was* glad they were there. It wouldn't have felt right if she'd had to leave without seeing them one more time. "I thought you had other things to do."

"We just told you that so we could surprise you. We did surprise you, didn't we?"

"You surprised me," Lisa said, beaming.

"Me too," Alex said. "I'm surprised, too. I really thought I could go for an afternoon, just *one* afternoon of my life, without seeing my twin sister."

Stevie grinned. "Well, there's always tomorrow," she said. "And that's something to look forward to, right?"

"Right," he said, grinning back.

Since she was closest to the outside, Callie went and got sodas for herself, Stevie, and Carole. When she rejoined the group, they were talking about everything in the world except the fact that Lisa was going to be gone for the summer and how much they were all going to miss one another.

She passed the drinks around and sat quietly at the end of the table. There wasn't much for her to say. She didn't really feel as if she belonged there. She wasn't anybody's best friend. It wasn't as if they minded her being there, but she'd come along because Stevie had offered to drive her to a tack shop after they left the airport. She was simply along for the ride.

". . . And don't forget to say hello to Skye."

"Skye? Skye who?" asked Alex.

"Don't pay any attention to him," Lisa said. "He's just jealous."

"You mean because Skye is a movie star?"

"And say hi to your father and the new baby. It must be exciting that you'll meet your sister."

"Well, of course, you've already met her, but now she's crawling, right? It's a whole different thing."

5

An announcement over the PA system brought their chatter to a sudden halt.

"It's my flight," Lisa said slowly. "They're starting to board and I've got to get through security and then to Gate . . . whatever."

"Fourteen," Alex said. "It comes after Gate Twelve. There are no thirteens in airports."

"Let's go."

"Here, I'll carry that."

"And I'll get this one . . ."

As Callie watched, Lisa hugged Carole and Stevie. Then she kissed Alex. Then she hugged her friends again. Then she turned to Alex.

"I think it's time for us to go," Carole said tactfully.

"Write or call every day," Stevie said.

"It's a promise," said Lisa. "Thanks for coming to the airport. You too, Callie."

Callie smiled and gave Lisa a quick hug before all the girls moved away, leaving her alone with Alex. They were going to miss her, but the girls had one another. Alex only had his lawns to mow. He needed the last minutes with Lisa.

"See you at home!" Stevie called over her shoulder, but she didn't think Alex heard. His attention was completely focused on one person.

Carole wiped a tear from her eye once they'd rounded a corner. "I'm going to miss her."

"Me too," said Stevie.

Carole turned to Callie. "It must be hard for you to understand," she said.

"Not really," said Callie. "I can tell you three are really close."

"We are," Carole said. "Best friends for a long time. We're practically inseparable." Even to her the words sounded exclusive and uninviting. If Callie noticed, she didn't say anything.

The three girls walked out of the terminal and found their way to Stevie's car. As she turned on the engine, Stevie was aware of an uncomfortable empty feeling. She really didn't like the idea of Lisa's being gone for the summer, and her own unhappiness was not going to be helped by a brother who was going to spend the entire time moping about his missing girlfriend. There had to be something that would make her feel better.

"Say, Carole, do you want to come along with us to the tack shop?" she asked.

"No, I can't," Carole said. "I promised I'd bring in the horses from the paddock before dark, so you can just drop me off at Pine Hollow. Anyway, aren't you due at work in an hour?"

Stevie glanced at her watch. Carole was right. Everything was taking longer than it was supposed to this afternoon.

"Don't worry," Callie said quickly. "We can go to the tack shop another time."

"You don't mind?" Stevie asked.

"No. I don't. Really," said Callie. "I don't want you to be late for work—either of you. If my parents decide to get a pizza for dinner again, I'm going to want it to arrive on time!"

Stevie laughed, but not because she thought anything was very funny. She wasn't about to forget the last time she'd delivered a pizza to Callie's family. In fact, she wished it hadn't happened, but it had. Now she had to find a way to face up to it.

As she pulled out of the airport parking lot, a plane roared overhead, rising into the brooding sky. *Maybe that's Lisa's plane,* she thought. The noise of its flight seemed to mark the beginning of a long summer.

The first splats of rain hit the windshield as Stevie paid their way out of the parking lot. By the time they were on the highway, it was raining hard. The sky had darkened to a steely gray. Streaks of lightning brightened it, only to be followed by thunder that made the girls jump.

The storm had come out of nowhere. Stevie flicked on the windshield wipers and hoped it would go right back to nowhere.

The sky turned almost black as the storm strengthened. Curtains of rain ripped across the windshield, pounding on the hood and roof of the car. The wipers flicked uselessly at the torrent.

8

"I hope Fez is okay," said Callie. "He hates thunder, you know."

"I'm not surprised," said Carole, trying to control her voice. It seemed to her that there were a lot of things Fez hated. He was as temperamental as any horse she had ever ridden.

Fez was one of the horses in the paddock. Carole didn't want to upset Callie by telling her that. If she told Callie he'd been turned out, Callie would wonder why he hadn't just been exercised. If she told Callie she'd exercised him, Callie might wonder if he was being overworked. Carole shook her head. What was it about Callie that made Carole so certain that whatever she said, it would be wrong? Why couldn't she say the one thing she really needed to say?

Still, Carole worked at Pine Hollow, and that meant taking care of the horses that were boarding there—and that meant keeping the owners happy.

"I'm sure Fez will be fine. Ben and Max will look after him," Carole said.

"I guess you're right," said Callie. "I know he can be difficult. Of course, you've ridden him, so you know that, too. I mean, that's obvious. But it's spirit, you see. Spirit is the key to an endurance specialist. He's got it, and I think he's got the makings of a champion. We'll work together this summer, and come fall . . . well, you'll see."

Spirit—yes, it was important in a horse. Carole knew that. She just wished she understood why it was that Fez's spirit was so irritating to her. She'd always thought of herself as someone who'd never met a horse she didn't like. Maybe it was the horse's owner . . .

"Uh-oh," said Stevie, putting her foot gently on the brake. "I think I got it going a little too fast there."

"You've got to watch out for that," Callie said. "My father says the police practically lie in wait for teenage drivers. They love to give us tickets. Well, they certainly had fun with me."

"You got a ticket?" Stevie asked.

"No, I just got a warning, but it was almost worse than a ticket. I was going four miles over the speed limit in our hometown. The policeman stopped me, and when he saw who I was, he just gave me a warning. Dad was furious—at me and at the officer, though he didn't say anything to the officer. He was angry at him because he thought someone would find out and say I'd gotten special treatment! I was only going four miles over the speed limit. Really. Even the officer said that. Well, it would have been easier if I'd gotten a ticket. Instead, I got grounded. Dad won't let me drive for three months. Of course, that's nothing compared to what happened to Scott last year."

"What happened to Scott?" Carole asked, suddenly curious about the driving challenges of the Forester children.

"Well, it's kind of a long story," said Callie. "But—"

"Wow! Look at that!" Stevie interrupted. There was an amazing streak of lightning over the road ahead. The dark afternoon brightened for a minute. Thunder followed instantly.

"Maybe we should pull off the road or something?" Carole suggested.

"I don't think so," said Stevie. She squinted through the windshield. "It's not going to last long. It never does when it rains this hard. We get off at the next exit anyway."

She slowed down some more and turned the wipers up a notch. She followed the driver in front of her, keeping a constant eye on the two red blurs of the car's taillights. She'd be okay as long as she could see them. The rain pelted the car so loudly that it was hard to talk. Stevie drove on cautiously.

Then, as suddenly as it had started, the rain stopped. Stevie spotted the sign for their exit, signaled, and pulled off to the right and up the ramp. She took a left onto the overpass and followed the road toward Willow Creek.

The sky was as dark as it had been, and there were signs that there had been some rain there, but nothing nearly as hard as the rain they'd left on the interstate. Stevie sighed with relief and switched the windshield wipers to a slower rate.

"I think I'll drop you off at Pine Hollow first," she said, turning onto the road that bordered the stable's property.

Pine Hollow's white fences followed the contour of the road, breaking the open, grassy hillside into a sequence of paddocks and fields. A few horses stood in the fields, swishing their tails. One bucked playfully and ran up a hill, shaking his head to free his mane in the wind. Stevie smiled. Horses always seemed to her the most welcoming sight in the world.

"Then I'll take Callie home," Stevie continued, "and after that I'll go over to Pizza Manor. I may be a few minutes late for work, but who orders pizza at five o'clock in the afternoon anyway?"

"Now, now," teased Carole. "Is that any way for you to mind your Pizza Manors?"

"Well, at least I have my hat with me," said Stevie. Or did she? She looked into the rearview mirror to see if she could spot it, and when that didn't do any good, she glanced over her shoulder. Callie picked it up and started to hand it to her.

"Here," she said. "We wouldn't want—Wow! I guess the storm isn't over yet!"

The sky had suddenly filled with a brilliant streak of lightning, jagged and pulsating, accompanied by an explosion of thunder.

It startled Stevie. She shrieked and turned her face back to the road. The light was so sudden and so bright that it blinded her for a second. The car swerved. Stevie braked. She clutched at the steering wheel and then realized she couldn't see because the rain was pelting even harder than before. She reached for the wiper control, switching it to its fastest speed.

There was something to her right! She saw something move, but she didn't know what it was.

"Stevie!" Carole cried.

"Look out!" Callie screamed from the backseat.

Stevie swerved to the left on the narrow road, hoping it would be enough. Her answer was a sickening jolt as the car slammed into something solid. The car spun around, smashing against the thing again. When the thing screamed, Stevie knew it was a horse. Then it disappeared from her field of vision. Once again, the car spun. It smashed against the guardrail on the left side of the road and tumbled up and over it as if the rail had never been there.

Down they went, rolling, spinning. Stevie could hear the screams of her friends. She could hear her own voice, echoing in the close confines of the car, answered by the thumps of the car rolling down the hillside into a gully. Suddenly the thumping stopped. The screams were stilled. The engine cut off. The wheels stopped spinning. And all Stevie could hear was the idle *slap, slap, slap* of her windshield wipers.

"Carole?" she whispered. "Are you okay?"

"I think so. What about you?" Carole answered.

"Me too. Callie? Are you okay?" Stevie asked.

There was no answer.

"Callie?" Carole echoed.

The only response was the girl's shallow breathing.

How could this have happened?

ONE

"Intermediate riding class will begin in the outdoor ring in five minutes!"

Carole could hear her voice echoing through the corridors of Pine Hollow Stables. It always gave her a kick to use the public-address system. With the flick of her finger, she could make a whole classful of girls and boys nervous. Nobody ever wanted to be late to class because nobody wanted to incur the wrath of a riding instructor.

Carole wasn't an instructor—yet. Though she did help the instructors from time to time, her official job that summer was to be the morning stable manager. She was at Pine Hollow from seven-thirty until noon every weekday, overseeing everything that happened, from ordering grain to assigning horses. Until she'd actually started the job, she'd had little idea of how much went on at Pine Hollow and how responsible she would be for it.

Carole had been a rider at the stable for about

seven years—before she owned her own horse, before her mother had died, long before her father had retired from the Marines. From the first time she'd ridden a horse, when she was four years old, she'd thought the finest job in the world would be getting paid to work with horses. Now, finally, she was doing that.

School was out for the summer, and until she went back as a junior in high school in September, she'd spend at least half of every day at Pine Hollow.

In the past, filling in for the stable manager at Pine Hollow had been a fairly routine task. Max Regnery owned the stable, as his father and grandfather had before him. His mother had been stable manager for years, and she had run the place smoothly, almost invisibly. That had all changed the past spring, however, when Mrs. Reg, as she was universally known, had decided to retire. She'd moved to Florida, leaving the stable in her son's hands, and he was relying on his students to do the work his mother used to do.

Everyone was stunned at how much work Mrs. Reg had magically accomplished. Carole and Denise McCaskill—the girl who was the afternoon manager that summer—were trying to do everything they could to take the huge load off Max's shoulders, but they were finding themselves as overwhelmed as he was.

Two little girls stormed into Carole's office. More accurately, one girl stormed in, chased by another.

"Carole, I want to ride the pinto today," whined Alexandra. "Justine rode him last week, so it's my turn now! You can't give me Nickel again. I had him last week and he misbehaved the whole time!"

"Don't even bother," Justine said to her classmate. "Carole gave me Patch, so I'm going to ride him and that's it. You shouldn't even ask."

"Carole?"

"You had trouble with Nickel last week because you weren't controlling him properly," Carole said calmly to Alexandra. "You won't have trouble with him this week because you will control him properly, but you will have trouble with Max if you don't get to class on time."

Alexandra glared. Justine smirked. Carole ignored them both. She flipped the switch on the PA system.

"Two minutes!" she said sharply. The girls fled from her office.

Carole wondered idly if she'd ever been as annoying as those two. She decided she hadn't been. Then she decided she *hoped* she hadn't been. She knew she'd liked some horses better than others, but as far as she could recall, there had never been a horse she hadn't liked. And there had never been a horse she hadn't been happy to ride.

No, she decided, in spite of the occasional irritating rider, she'd found the perfect job.

Ben, one of the stable hands, came halfway into the office, pausing nearer the door than the desk. Ben was like that. It was as if he didn't really want to commit to a conversation, but there was something he had to say.

"The stall is ready for that new horse," he told Carole. "Almost, I mean."

"Oh, right," Carole said. She opened her drawer and took out the bronze nameplate that had come from the engraver that morning. FEZ, it read. She walked over to give it to Ben. With anybody else, Carole would have thought it was rude to wait to be handed something. With Ben, though, it was different. He was shy and never seemed to feel as if he belonged. He was as reluctant to go into Carole's office as he was to go into Max's.

The only place Ben seemed comfortable, in fact, was standing next to or sitting on a horse. Carole had never known anyone with as sure a touch as Ben had. He never hesitated with horses the way he did with humans. He could look horses straight in the eye and they'd do what he wanted them to do. People were another story.

Even if Carole had trouble understanding Ben

18

as a person, she had no trouble understanding him as a horse handler. She could watch him work with horses for hours on end. She did, in fact. From her desk, she could see him while he did his chores around the stable, grooming, tending, training, healing, and caring for the horses that lived there. He might stammer trying to utter a complete sentence to a person, but he seemed able to convey a whole world to a horse.

Carole had watched him soothe a frightened horse through an entire vet visit the week before. Anyone else would have had to twitch the horse, squeezing its nose and upper lip with a chain loop that irritated and distracted it so much that it wouldn't notice what the vet was doing. Ben didn't use the twitch, though. He stood by the horse's head, holding it on a short lead. Ben patted its cheek and whispered into its ear. The horse never budged—even when Judy Barker, the vet, took a blood sample. Ben was amazing.

"Must be some special horse," Ben said, looking at the small bronze plaque in his hand. Briefly Carole wondered what had instigated this rush of chatter from him, but then she realized it was the bronze plaque itself and Max's insistence that the stall be completely prepared before the horse's arrival.

"Some kind of VIP?"

"Uh, sort of," Carole said.

"Horse or owner?" Ben asked.

Carole laughed. Ben wouldn't be anywhere near as impressed with an owner's pedigree as he would with a horse's. In this case, however, both were impressive. Carole picked up the folder Max had filled with information about the horse and its rider.

"The horse is an Arabian endurance specialist. He's got a lot of medals and ribbons to his credit. He deserves all the work you've put into the stall, plus the brass nameplate."

"And the owner?"

"Actually, she's not the owner. She's renting Fez for the summer, option to buy and all that. Her name is Callie Forester. She's sixteen years old. She's won a dozen ribbons of her own."

"Never heard of her," Ben said dismissively.

"Not here. She's just moved here from somewhere on the West Coast." Carole ran her finger down the sheet of paper, scanning the notes Max had taken from Callie's parents when they'd made the arrangements. "Oh, I get it," Carole said. "Her father is a congressman. I guess he just got elected last year and Callie was finishing out the school year back home. She's here for the summer. Maybe longer, though it's not clear how long they've leased Fez for."

"Okay," said Ben. He backed out of her office, slinking into the shadows of the stable. That was just like him. He'd heard enough and wanted to flee to the safety of the horses that filled the stalls of Pine Hollow.

Carole knew she was horse-crazy, and she knew it was a trait she'd have all her life. Ben was horse-crazy, too. She liked that about him. Odd as he could be, that single fact about him helped bring them together.

Carole glanced at her watch. This was going to be a busy morning, and she didn't have time to waste thinking about Ben Marlow. One of the things that was going to make it busy was that she had to find someone to cover for her the day after next. She and her best friends, Lisa Atwood and Stevie Lake, had a long-standing date to go for a trail ride.

Stevie, Lisa, and Carole were so close that Carole couldn't remember a time when the other two hadn't been her friends—just the way she couldn't remember a time when she wasn't horse-crazy. Several years earlier they'd formed a club, and it remained a bond between them. It wasn't the formality of the club—not that The Saddle Club had ever been very formal—that kept them together; it was their common love of horses.

The girls were very different from one another and always had been. Carole was acknowledged to be the most serious about horses but the least serious about anything else. Sometimes she thought the only thing that really mattered to her was horses. Sometimes that didn't seem like a bad thing. Now, as she grew older, she was even more convinced that horses would be her life. Just two more years of high school and she could enter a university equine studies program. That was what she wanted more than anything.

While Carole was serious about horses, Stevie sometimes seemed to have trouble being serious about anything. She had outgrown her passion for practical jokes, and her friends were more than a little relieved that she'd given up playing pranks on her brothers. Stevie had three of them: Chad, now in college; her twin brother Alex; and her younger brother, Michael. When the Lakes started playing jokes on each other, things often got out of hand. But everyone had calmed down, or perhaps just grown up, now. Still, Stevie had an irrepressible spirit that tended more toward trouble than practicality.

One constant factor in Stevie's life was her boyfriend, Phil Marsten. They had met at riding camp one summer when they were twelve and in junior high school. They'd fallen in love then and had only gotten closer since. Both Carole and Lisa liked Phil, and he liked them, too.

In fact, the girls were such good friends that it would be difficult for anyone, even a boyfriend, to come between them, but that was put to the test when Stevie's brother Alex and Lisa suddenly fell in love. Carole and Stevie had been there when it happened, and neither had seen it coming. Apparently, neither had Lisa and Alex. The girls had been at dinner at the Lakes' house. In the midst of a raucous conversation about politics and the undesirable high jinks of certain politicians in nearby Washington, D.C., Lisa had asked Alex to hand her the water.

Alex reached for the pitcher and picked it up. He turned to pour water into Lisa's glass, but before he could do it, their eyes met, and it was as if they were seeing one another for the first time. Alex began pouring the water—right onto the table. That in and of itself didn't mean much. What did tell Stevie and Carole that something important was happening was that Lisa didn't notice . . . until she picked up her empty glass to drink out of it. And at that moment, Lisa's life changed for the good, forever.

Lisa had been having a rough time dealing with her parents' divorce. There had been several years of squabbling and ugly silence in the Atwood home. Then, as Lisa began to think she was accustomed to it, everything got turned upside down again. Her parents told her one morning at breakfast that their marriage was over. Within a month, Mr. Atwood had moved to California. A year after that, when the divorce was final, he'd remarried. Not long after that, Lisa found that she had a baby sister named Lily in addition to a stepmother named Evelyn. She liked Evelyn. She even loved Lily. But so many changes in such a short time were confusing, and nobody knew that better than her best friends.

Lisa, always the coolheaded clear thinker of the trio, had gone through a period when she was as capable of forgetting her coat as Carole or as likely to get into hot water at school as Stevie. All that ended the day she fell in love with Alex. It was as if he were the missing piece—or, as Lisa sometimes thought of him, the missing peace—in her life.

At first Stevie had worried about her best friend's dating her brother, afraid that she'd be forced to choose between them, but that hadn't happened. And now, six months later, Lisa and Alex were still as much in love as before, and Lisa had managed to revert to her normal reliable, calm, logical self. Her friends were glad to have her back.

Other things were also different than they had been when the three girls had been in junior high school. Back then, they seemed to be able to meet at Pine Hollow every day after school and spend all day on the weekends together, at Pony Club meetings, riding, studying, grooming, and just being around the horses. Now there were huge assignments at school, jobs after school, family obligations, and time spent with boyfriends and even with study groups. Nothing changed the way the girls felt about one another, but life had interfered with their schedule.

Except for the day after next. They'd promised each other one trail ride, just for themselves—no boyfriends, no parents, no interruptions. It was the last chance they'd have to be together before Lisa left for the summer. She was going to California to be with her father, Lily, and Evelyn until September.

Carole hated the fact that Lisa would be gone. Stevie didn't like it any better. Alex was broken-hearted, and Lisa's mother was furious.

And that was the main reason nobody wanted to talk to Lisa about her decision. Her mother had been very badly hurt by the divorce. She had always been a fragile woman, devoted to trivial details, and now her world was shattered. A trivial world shatters easily, Carole had observed. The woman who once obsessed about Lisa's proper upbringing, dancing lessons, painting lessons, piano instruction, and posture had now withdrawn from the whole process, leaving Lisa to her own devices.

Lisa's devices and resources were considerable. She looked after herself and was a straight-A student. She also took on the responsibility of looking after her mother, shopping and cooking for the two of them regularly. No wonder Lisa wanted to go to California for the summer. She needed a rest.

Carole's reverie about her friends was broken by the familiar sound of a pair of crutches thumping along the hallway toward her office.

"Hi, Emily!" she called out.

"Hello, Carole," Emily Williams said. Then the girl peered around the corner into the office, smiling warmly. "Greetings! Anything going on?"

"Lots," Carole told her. "And before you ask, the answer is yes, you can help."

"That's what I get for my generosity of spirit," Emily said, slipping into the chair in front of Carole's desk. She propped her crutches against the chair, crossed her arms in front of her, looked Carole straight in the eye, and said, "Shoot."

"Two things: First of all, can you cover for me in the office day after tomorrow?"

"Of course," Emily said. "As long as I don't have to sort out which of the beginning riders gets Nickel and which gets Patch."

"I'll make a list of horse assignments and leave it for you," Carole said. "I really mostly need you on the phone."

"I'm good at the phone," said Emily.

"You're good at everything," Carole said.

"Don't think you can get off easy just because of those." Carole pointed to the crutches.

"I've tried, and it doesn't work," Emily said. Both girls laughed. There were a lot of things Emily had tried to do with the crutches she'd had all her life, but getting sympathy was not one of them. She'd been born with cerebral palsy and wore leg braces, besides walking with crutches. Sometimes if she got really tired, she used a wheelchair. None of that seemed to matter, though, because once Emily had made up her mind to do something, she always managed to do it. And she made up her mind to do just about everything.

Emily had her own horse, a well-trained one she called PC. She rode him every bit as skillfully as the other riders at Pine Hollow rode their horses. She'd won as many ribbons as other fully abled riders, and nobody doubted for a second that she had earned those ribbons. Emily was as devoted to her horse and to riding as Carole and her other friends—more, perhaps. She referred to PC as her great equalizer. When she was in his saddle, there was no thump of crutches. There was no telltale awkwardness in her gait. She could move as quickly as her friends. She could turn, run, and jump just as well as they could. Best of all, they were as happy about it as she was.

"And the other thing?" Emily asked.

"Oh, right. Well, we've got a new boarder arriving this morning. Can you cover the desk while I help with the unloading? According to the notes, he's supposed to be a little tough to handle."

"Sure," said Emily. "But what about Ben?"

"He'll be there, too," Carole said. "I just want to be sure we give this fellow a great Pine Hollow welcome."

"Some kind of VIP?" Emily asked.

"I guess so," said Carole. "The horse is named Fez. The owner is Callie Forester."

"The congressman's daughter?" Emily asked.

"Yeah, how'd you know?"

"I read all about her in one of my horse magazines. Didn't you see the article? I guess not, huh—but anyway, sure, she's won like a zillion ribbons for endurance riding. Fez is a champion in his own right. The junior endurance world has been waiting for these two to pair up. It was a long article, mostly about how difficult it is for her having to move now that her father's been elected."

"It can be tough," said Carole. "Sort of like being an instant princess. Dad met these people at one of those black-tie dinners he goes to—"

"Spare me *Lifestyles of the Rich and Overprivileged*," said Emily.

"I guess," said Carole. "But it can't be easy to

be in the public eye the way a congressman's daughter is. And think of all the boring political dinners and conventions and things like that. Must be hard to find time to ride."

"She finds time, trust me," said Emily. "The article was all about how she spends hours a day conditioning herself and her horse. It also said she has a brother who is supposed to be this hotshot kid, president of his high-school debate team, most likely to succeed—like his father. The brother's name is Scott, I think.

"And the horse—well, she only rode him for a few minutes before she knew this was the horse she wanted. Her parents made arrangements to rent him for the summer, and they expect to buy him in September if he lives up to his promise. He's spirited, all right. The woman who wrote the article spent most of her time talking about flared nostrils. In the photographs, his ears were back, flat against his head. I bet he's going to be a handful."

"Well, we'll do our best to make him welcome and comfortable," Carole said.

She thought she sounded like an innkeeper. She had every intention of doing whatever was necessary to make their famous guest and his equally famous rider very comfortable. Usually Carole didn't notice much about riders and horses except how the horses were doing and how the riders rode. For some reason, Fez and Callie were making her nervous, even before she'd met them.

Carole had met congressmen and their daughters before. Pine Hollow was in a suburb of Washington, and there were a lot of people from the government around. It was nothing new. She'd met championship horses before, too. She'd even ridden them. She'd never met a horse she didn't like, and more important, she'd never met a horse she couldn't make like and trust her. What was the big deal here? Maybe it was that, for the first time, she was truly, officially, working at Pine Hollow. She wasn't just one of the riders at the stable, she *was* the stable. The opportunities for error seemed vast. She shook off the thought. Fez would be there shortly. There was no big deal about it. He was a horse, just like any other horse. He'd be fine—and so would she.

"Is that a horse van I hear?" Emily asked, sitting up in her chair so that she could see through the office window.

Carole looked, too. Emily was right. Fez was there. Time to become the welcoming innkeeper, directing her newest guest into the stable.

TWO

"Welcome to Pine Hollow," Carole said to the van driver. "My name is Carole Hanson, and—"

"Let's just get this baby unloaded. We're late and it's all because of him. Here are the papers."

The driver shoved a clipboard at Carole and went to the back of the van, where he started opening the latch. Even before the door was open, Carole knew they were in for some trouble. She could hear the horse stomping on the floor. He whinnied. The sound conveyed both irritation and restlessness.

She looked at the papers. Everything seemed to be in order. Fez had come from a farm in West Virginia. He'd been traveling about six hours, and he obviously didn't like it. Some horses took traveling in stride, settled into new homes easily, adjusted to a variety of riders, and did their best for each one. Nothing that Carole had learned so far about Fez made her think he was that kind of horse.

While she finished checking the paperwork, Ben stepped up to give the van driver a hand. It was almost like opening a Christmas present—one that really wanted to get out of the box.

First the outer doors were unlatched and swung open. Then the driver lowered the ramp. Next came the inner door, the stall enclosure inside the van. And there was Fez—or at least Fez's rump. His tail switched agitatedly.

Ben hopped up into the van and clipped a lead rope onto the Arabian's halter.

"You're going to have to mask him," the driver said. "It took that, and more, to get him on. Lord knows what it'll take to get him off."

Carole and Ben each took one side of Fez, guiding him every step of the way, and every step was painful—at least for Carole. With Fez's first step, he managed to give Carole a solid kick in her thigh. She could feel her flesh welting up into a swollen mass and knew it would be a beauty of a bruise.

"Thanks, boy," she said gently. It wasn't what she really wanted to say, but losing her temper with a horse had never done any good. She patted Fez on the neck, hoping to soothe him. He eyed her warily, and then Ben slipped a hood over his head.

The theory was that if a horse couldn't see where he was going, he would follow a lead willingly, since it was probably more reliable than information he was getting with his eyes. Fez apparently wasn't confident about Carole's and Ben's ability to lead him, so he remained almost as balky with the mask as he had been without it.

"Time for a bribe," Carole said. She pulled a carrot out of her pocket and held it in front of his nose. Fez sniffed and then took it up in his teeth, nipping Carole's hand as he did so. Carole suspected he'd done it on purpose, but she still didn't lose her temper. She had a bruised leg and a sore hand and all they'd managed to do was to get the horse to the top of the ramp.

It took another half hour before the job was done. Step by step, carrot by carrot, sore finger by swollen toe, Carole and Ben finally had Fez on the ground and removed his mask. He thanked them by rearing. Carole wasn't sorry when she could finally ask Ben to take the horse to his stall while she finished up the paperwork. Ben said nothing as he led the balky gelding into the stable. A lot of horses were difficult to get into and out of vans. Few remained cranky when they were on solid ground. Fez appeared to be an exception to that rule. Ben patted him and spoke to him, but Fez's ears remained pinned to his head. Still, he followed Ben.

"Whew, he's a handful," Carole said. "I guess it'll take a few days for him to settle in."

"Don't count on it," said the driver. He took his own copy of the documentation and left Carole wondering what he knew that she didn't.

She could have checked to see if Ben needed a hand, but she headed straight back to the office. Callie was bound to show up in a few minutes, and Carole wanted to be sure her file was complete and all the stable's records were properly prepared. She didn't want to disappoint the congressman's daughter. Each of Pine Hollow's boarders had a notebook in which all the paperwork was kept—everything from transport records to immunizations to feeding schedules to exercise records. There was a lot of information to enter already. She sat down at her desk and took out a new notebook, plus dividers, labels, and forms. She had barely begun to type up the labels before her first interruption.

"Guess what I got!"

It was Stevie, running into the office breathless with excitement. It could only mean one thing.

"You passed?"

"You bet I did!" Stevie said. "I am now a fully licensed driver. Here, look!" she said, holding out the brand-new license. It looked a lot like the one Carole already had.

"It's beautiful!" Carole said, with only a hint of sarcasm. She'd long ago learned that sometimes the easiest way to get along with Stevie was to agree with her—especially when she was being totally irrational. Actually, considering the accomplishment, Carole didn't really think Stevie was being all *that* irrational. A new driver's license was something to be happy about.

"And Alex?" Carole asked. Stevie and Alex were taking their tests on the same day.

"Well, it was a near thing, but he passed, too," Stevie conceded. Carole strongly suspected it hadn't been a near thing at all. Stevie used to spend a lot of time competing with all three of her brothers. Their house still bore the scars of a few water balloons gone astray. Now that they were older, they no longer fought as they had in the past, but it was still sometimes difficult for Stevie to admit in public that her twin was actually related to her. The only thing he'd ever done that she boasted about on his behalf was to fall in love with her friend Lisa.

"He told me he started to turn the wheels the wrong way in the middle of his three-point turn, but he corrected it before they said anything. Can you imagine? Blowing a three-point turn?"

"And you?" Carole asked.

"It went like a breeze," Stevie said. "When

they asked me what the rearview mirror was for, I explained that it was for putting on lipstick without lowering the visor. No problem."

Carole almost believed her, but then Stevie had been able to pull her leg as long as they'd known each other.

"And the horn is to let your friends know you're waiting, right?"

"Exactly," said Stevie. "Now, do you want to go for a ride?"

"Well, sure," Carole said. "I'll be done here in another hour, and I was planning to exercise Starlight then. Why don't you go groom Belle and tack them both up? We can be on the trail right after I'm done. We can't take a long ride, but it should be fun—"

"Actually, I meant in my car. I don't have time to ride Belle today. I saw this ad in the paper—"

"Oh," Carole said, disappointed. It would have been fun to ride with Stevie.

"No, it's really good news," Stevie said, sensing Carole's disappointment. "See, now that Alex and I have our licenses, we can both drive the car Chad left when he went to college. We've worked out a schedule for it, and it means I can get a job. Actually, I just about *have* to get a job, because Mom and Dad are making us pay the insurance and that's a lot of money, which is why Alex is going to be spending the summer breaking his back mowing lawns. Anyway, I heard that Pizza Manor is looking for a delivery person because Alex's friend, Elroy, quit last night and the manager gets in at eleven today and he'll be desperate for a new driver. Who could be more perfect than yours truly?"

"Nobody," Carole agreed. "You are, without a doubt, the ideal person for the job. Go for it."

"Well, the interview isn't for another forty-five minutes, so I thought I'd visit with you."

Carole looked at the pile of work on her desk, including the notebook of Fez's records. Time spent with Stevie was rarely time spent doing a job, much as she would have liked to talk with her friend—even to hear more details about her driving test. But she had to work.

"Look, I can't," she said. "I'm sorry, but the new horse just came in, and I've got to get some paperwork done before the owner arrives. But the good news is that I've asked Emily to cover for me the day after tomorrow so you and Lisa and I can go on our farewell ride before you-know-what happens."

"I sure do know what," Stevie said. "It's the only topic of discussion at my house these days. Well, I mean it's the only thing Alex wants to talk about. I'm sorry Lisa's going away for the summer, but I guess I understand it. It's her father, after all.

"That's great that Emily can cover for you. We should be able to be out of here by ten o'clock or so."

"That's what I thought," said Carole. "And we won't have to worry about your new job meaning you can't go. There aren't too many people who order pizzas for breakfast."

"I think we'll be safe on that score, *if* I get the job."

"Job? What job?" Lisa entered the office.

"I got my license, and now I'm going to apply for a job at Pizza Manor."

"Oh, that's great!" said Lisa. "By any chance, did anybody else in your family get a license today?"

"Gee, who could she be asking about?" Stevie said.

"Both your parents have licenses," Carole said. "And we all know Chad does. So that leaves the dog, right?"

"Only if the dog is named Alex," said Lisa. "Did he pass?"

"Yeah, he did," Stevie assured her. "And that means he can get to all those lawns he's going to mow while you're away. You won't have to worry about him getting into trouble at all. He'll be too tired every night to do anything."

"I wasn't worried about that," Lisa said. "I know you'll look after my interests."

"Actually," Stevie said, "you are the one thing we almost never talk about. He used to confide in me about his girlfriends, but not about you. Oh, sure, he's been mooning around the house, complaining about you going away for the whole summer, but he never says anything really personal. He assumes you talk to me about him."

"Which of course I don't," said Lisa.

"That's the problem with having your brother date your best friend. I'm missing out on all the good dope from two people I used to be able to count on!"

Lisa flopped into the other chair in Carole's office. Carole glanced at Fez's incomplete notebook and the pile of other paperwork that awaited her, but for the moment, her friends' concerns were more important. Fez could wait a few minutes.

"This is the worst!" Carole said. "Stevie and I are going to miss you, and Alex is going to be miserable, and that'll make Stevie miserable, and you know that when Stevie's miserable, the whole world is miserable."

"Aw, come on," Lisa said, a little bite in her voice. "It's not going to be that long. I didn't ask my parents to get a divorce. I didn't tell Dad to fall in love with someone who lives in California. I didn't choose to have my life split in half."

"Easy, easy," Carole said. "We're just venting. I guess none of us much likes the whole situation, so maybe we'd better stop talking about it."

"Or else we could look on the positive side," Stevie suggested.

"And that is?"

"You're going to spend a whole summer in sunny Southern California. You'll certainly get to see Skye, and that's always lots of fun."

"He's pretty busy," Lisa said.

"Starring in another movie?" asked Carole. Skye Ransom was an actor the girls had known for a long time. They'd met him by accident—his accident—when he'd fallen off a horse. They'd helped him out, and they'd been friends ever since.

"No, it's not a movie," said Stevie. "It's a television series. A contemporary series set on a horse ranch. He's been cast as the young romantic lead. All the girls who come to the ranch fall in love with him."

"That's more like fact than fiction," Lisa remarked. Then she realized that her boyfriend's sister might not find that very funny. "Not that he's my type, mind you. Personally, I prefer the lawn mower type to the handsome young star type."

"I'll be sure to tell Alex you said that," Stevie promised.

"No, don't," said Lisa. "I don't think he likes to hear anything about Skye Ransom. He can't help being insecure, but, honestly, he has nothing to be insecure about. Skye's just a friend."

"Even with all the razzle-dazzle of Hollywood?" Carole asked.

"Especially with all that," Lisa said. "It's a nice place to visit, you know?"

"But you wouldn't want to live there?"

"Never," Lisa said. "Absolutely never."

"Well, that's good enough for me," Carole said. She pulled a pile of papers in front of her.

"I think that's a hint," Lisa said. She stood up. Stevie stood up as well, then glanced at her watch.

"Oh, look! It's time for me to go to Pizza Manor. Do you want to come along for a ride?" she asked Lisa.

"Sure," Lisa agreed.

"You can't apply for the job," Stevie said, suddenly a little concerned that super-organized Lisa might beat her to the job she was counting on, just to avoid being away from Alex.

"Don't worry. I'm hungry. I'll have some veggie pizza while you wow the manager with your driving skills, your reliability, and your sparkling personality."

41

"Deal," Stevie said.

The two of them said good-bye to Carole and headed out.

Carole opened up the notebook, and on the top of the first page, she wrote *Fez*.

THREE

"Stevie, relax. You don't have to hold the wheel so tightly," said Lisa.

"I do kind of clutch it, don't I?" Stevie acknowledged. She tried to relax her hands. Her knuckles changed from milky white to a healthy flesh color.

"Are you nervous when you drive?" Lisa asked uneasily.

"No, not really," said Stevie. "But you know, it's kind of new, with my driver's license and all. I don't want to make any mistakes."

"You won't," Lisa said. "All you have to do is to keep a few things in mind. Keep your hands steady, your foot limber, and your eyes moving, and concentrate on where you're going."

"Sounds just like riding a horse," Stevie said.

"I guess so, and, like riding a horse, it's a matter of being able to focus on fifteen or twenty things at once, like that double-parked—*Stevie!*"

Stevie swerved to the left, avoiding the double-

43

parked car by a good tenth of an inch. Lisa felt her heart slowly settle back into her chest.

"No problem," Stevie assured her.

"Right," Lisa agreed. She decided not to distract Stevie by giving her any more instructions until they reached Pizza Manor. It hadn't been all that long ago that Lisa had gotten her own driver's license. She was a year older than Stevie, a year ahead of her in school, and a year more experienced as a driver. Her own first day had been spent driving her friends to and from every place in town where they'd wanted to go. It had been wonderful fun, even if they had never gone above fifteen miles per hour. Now, a year later, she was an able and confident driver. Soon enough Stevie would be, too.

Stevie managed to complete the trip without any more near misses or even not-so-near ones. She looked at her watch. She was right on time for her interview. Being on time had never been one of her strong points. Perhaps getting her driver's license and being on time for an appointment on the same day meant she was turning over a new leaf. She took a nice deep breath. Everything was going to be wonderful. She would get the job. She was sure of it. She and Lisa walked in together.

Pizza Manor was a small restaurant in the shopping center near Pine Hollow. The shopping center had few things to recommend it. Besides Pizza Manor, which was a relatively new addition, there were a handful of other stores that seemed to change regularly: a shoe store that became a record store; a gift shop that turned into a liquor store and then into a dry cleaner's. The two things there that never seemed to change were the supermarket and TD's. TD's stood for Tastee Delight. It was an ice cream shop that Stevie, Lisa, and Carole had been going to as long as they'd been friends. They still liked crowding into their favorite booth every now and then for something sweet and gooey.

"Welcome to Pizza Manor. May I help you?" said the smiling girl behind the counter.

The girl was Polly Giacomin. She rode at Pine Hollow with Stevie and Lisa. It felt funny to have her offer to wait on them.

"Hi, Polly," Lisa said. "I'll have a slice of veggie pizza and a small diet soda."

"M'kay. . . . Stevie?"

"I'll have an interview."

Polly smiled. She knew Stevie.

"So you passed the test?"

Stevie nodded.

"The manager's in the back. I'll let him know you're here. He's been tearing out his hair all day because Elroy quit last night. He's afraid he's going to have to make the deliveries himself. Just smile nicely, show him your license, and you'll get the job."

She drew a soda and slipped a slice of pizza onto a red-and-white-checked paper plate, then handed them to Lisa. "Hang on a second," she said to Stevie.

Lisa took her lunch to a nearby table and sat down to eat and wait.

Stevie didn't move, afraid that she couldn't. The day had been something else. In spite of what she'd said to her friends, her driving test hadn't gone *that* smoothly. She loved driving. She'd loved it from the first moment her father had let her sit behind the wheel the day she'd gotten her learner's permit. She loved the powerful feel of the car, knowing that she and she alone was in charge. It was similar to but not exactly the same as riding, since the car was only a machine and not a living, responsive animal. But what a machine it was—big, noisy, shiny, expensive. It could take her anywhere. She didn't have to feed it or groom it. She only had to give it gas—and pay the insurance.

She'd almost blown it, too. Or maybe she hadn't. The man who gave her the driving test had sat stony-faced during the entire ordeal, not speaking except to issue instructions. She had no idea what she'd done wrong or right. She only knew that in the end, it had worked. Had he noticed that she didn't really look over her shoulder when she pulled out of the parking place? Had he been aware that she was a little bit over the center line when she was making a left turn? Maybe he had, or maybe he hadn't. She'd passed. That was the important thing.

And now here she was, ready for another test—this time to get a job. Who was she kidding? She barely knew how to drive. She didn't know the first thing about the restaurant business except that she was a pretty good eater. She was usually late for things, but she'd made it that day. She was wearing an old pair of jeans and a wrinkled shirt, and she hadn't combed her hair, and she probably smelled of horses because she'd stopped by Pine Hollow, *and* she'd never had a real job before.

Suddenly a man was standing in front of her on the other side of the counter. He was stocky and had a mustache. He had combed his thinning hair from one ear to the other to make stripes of hair across the top of his head.

"You here about the delivery job?" he asked.

"Me?" Stevie asked, glancing over her shoulder.

"Yeah, you."

"Oh, right, yes," said Stevie, offering her hand. He shook it.

"Polly said there was a boy here, too. Steve something."

"That's me. Except I'm not a boy. I'm Stevie Lake—it's short for Stephanie, but don't tell anybody that."

"My daughter's named Stephanie," he said.

I've blown it, Stevie thought. *I've made him think I'm crazy and I've insulted his daughter. He's not going to hire me. In fact, nobody will ever hire me. I can't really drive and—*

"You have a license?"

"Yes."

"May I see it, please?"

"Oh, sure," Stevie said, fishing it out of her purse. She handed it to him.

"Kind of rushing things, aren't you?" he said.

What had she done wrong now?

"Sorry?"

"I don't think I've ever seen a license as fresh and new as this," he said. "It's like holding a newborn baby. Did you come straight here, or did you stop to show your friends?"

"Um, my friends," Stevie said, pointing to Lisa, who was calmly eating her pizza, totally unaware of the fact that Stevie was making an idiot of herself just out of earshot. Then Stevie looked at the man. It took her another two seconds to realize he was teasing her.

"I would have come straight here, sir, but I

thought it would impress you more if you could see how much business I would bring in for you."

"That's just one customer," the man said.

"Right, but she's *very* hungry."

"Okay. Come on back to my office. You've got to fill out an application and tell me a little bit about yourself. So far, all I know is that the Commonwealth of Virginia thinks you're an adequate driver, and you've got a smart mouth on you. Anything else?"

"No sir, that's me in a nutshell," Stevie assured him.

She followed him, wondering what she was getting herself into.

FOUR

Carole heard a knock at her office door. At least she'd been able to finish putting the papers in Fez's notebook before the next interruption. She looked up.

A very handsome guy leaned in the doorway, looking back at her. She smiled automatically in response to the smile he gave her.

"Is Callie here?" he asked.

"Forester? Uh, no," Carole said. "She hasn't been here yet. But her horse is here. Would you like to see him?"

"No thank you," the boy said, smiling wryly. "I hear enough about him to satisfy any curiosity I have."

That was all the hint Carole needed. Only a nonriding brother could respond that way to his sister's horse.

"You must be Scott," Carole said. "I'm Carole Hanson, morning stable manager for the summer."

He took her hand and shook it. "Well, I'm glad I didn't come in the afternoon or the fall. Otherwise I would have missed the opportunity to meet you."

"Instead, you've only missed your sister. I don't know when she's going to be here. Would you like me to give her a message?"

"No, I'm waiting for her. I'm supposed to pick her up after she's checked on Fez. My father is dropping her off on his way into town, but he can't wait for her, so I've got chauffeur duty—which is an honor I accept in return for being able to use the car."

"Oh, it's station-wagon bingo, huh?" Carole teased.

Scott laughed and took a chair across the desk from her. "Don't you know it. You must have brothers and sisters, too."

"No, I'm an only," Carole told him. "And there's no argument over the car in my house. My father gets it when he wants it. See, he's a retired Marine."

"Can't be any harder to argue with than a man who makes his living as a politician."

"I think you've got me there," Carole said. "But when he says 'Ten-*shun!*' . . . Well, enough about that." She stood up from her desk. "I was about to go look in on Fez, so if you want to come with me, you're welcome, or you can stay here."

Scott stood up. "Oh, sure," he said. "I'll come along. I guess I might as well have a face to put with this superhorse after all."

He followed Carole down the wide aisle that separated the horses' stalls. Fez's stall was on the other side of the stable. Carole took the opportunity to introduce Scott to a lot of horses as they went, including her own, Starlight, and Stevie's horse, Belle. If Scott didn't like horses—and he certainly hadn't given Carole the impression that he did—he was pretty good at feigning interest. He patted them warmly and asked good questions. He asked Carole why it was so important to his sister that her horse was an Arab.

"I mean, your horse—um, Starlight?" he said. Carole nodded. "You said he's part Thoroughbred. I thought they were the best. Why wouldn't she want a Thoroughbred, then? I mean, if there's one thing you can count on about Callie, it's that she wants the best when it comes to horses."

"Me too," Carole said. "But *best* is a relative term. I wanted a horse I could ride for pleasure and competition. Starlight is fine in a ring and a great jumper, but he's no match for most Arabs on an endurance ride. Thoroughbreds were developed for their speed. Where they're 'best' is at the racetrack. Arabs were bred for desert life. They're surefooted and powerful, and they can go for long periods without water. They have stamina and a lot of heart. That's why they tend to stand out in endurance competitions. Now, quarter horses, for instance, are faster than Thoroughbreds—for short distances. They're like sprinters."

"I think I'm getting this," Scott said. "An Arab is like a marathon runner; you want a Thoroughbred in the four-forty, but a quarter horse in the hundred-meter dash."

"You're a quick study," Carole said.

"And you're a good teacher," Scott countered.

Carole blushed. She actually blushed. And she felt more than a little dumb about it. She hoped he didn't notice. Scott was friendly and really cute. He was easy to talk to, he was interested in what she had to say—or at least very good at pretending he was—and he seemed like a good listener, too. It made her all the more pleased that Callie was going to be riding with them. If Scott was so nice, then Callie was bound to be, too. That was something to look forward to.

Ben was still working with Fez when they got to his stall. The horse seemed only marginally happier to be there than he had when he'd arrived, and Carole suspected that all of the improvement was due to Ben's presence. He was holding Fez gently but firmly by a lead line and currying his neck when they approached. Horses

53

liked to be groomed. The coat on Fez's neck was already shiny and clean. Clearly, it didn't need one more second of attention, but Fez needed a lot more attention to calm him down. Ben understood that and was doing what was necessary.

"Scott, I'd like you to meet Ben Marlow . . ."

"Pleased to meet you," Scott said, offering Ben his hand.

Ben regarded it quickly and then nodded instead. He had his hands full with Fez and wasn't about to let go. Carole thought it wouldn't have hurt for him to say as much. Scott pulled back his hand.

"I guess this must be the fabled Fez," Scott said.

Ben nodded again.

"Um, he's been fussy since he got here," Carole said. "Ben's trying to give him the old Pine Hollow welcome and help him settle in. I think he doesn't like traveling much."

Scott leaned up against one of the pillars, propping his elbow over his head and leaning easily. Carole remembered how he'd taken to the chair in her office, immediately making himself at home. She was struck by the fact that Scott managed to make himself comfortable wherever he was, and as a result she was comfortable, too—as long as he didn't compliment her too much.

"Is that one of those qualities of various breeds you were talking about?" Scott asked.

"Oh, I don't think so," Carole said. "Every horse has its own personality, regardless of breed. Some horses love to be vanned and walk up and down the ramp without any trouble. There are a couple of horses here who try to get on every van that comes into the yard. Others hate it, and every time they go anyplace, it's a struggle. Your friend Fez here falls into that category."

Carole became aware that the two of them were talking around Ben—almost as if he weren't there. Since he was, however, she thought it would be polite to bring him into the conversation.

"Ben, why don't you tell Scott what we had to go through to get this guy off the van?"

"Oh, it wasn't too bad," Ben said. "Just had to persuade him. He's okay now."

That was it. That was all Ben intended to say. He could be infuriating, Carole thought. What was the matter with sharing the tale with Scott? Some people would have enjoyed hearing about the mask and the bribes. Scott was one of them, Carole was sure.

"We kind of took the carrot-and-stick approach," Carole said. "Literally. Except we didn't dangle the carrot off a stick. I held the carrots close enough for him to be able to sniff them—

which he had to do because he had a mask over his eyes."

"You blindfolded him? You mean he's so dumb he couldn't figure out where he was going?"

Carole had never actually thought of it in those terms. "We hope so," she said. That made Scott laugh. His laugh was so infectious that it made her laugh, too. It didn't, however, make Ben laugh. He simply kept up his work, grooming Fez.

Fez's ears perked up suddenly, and then Carole heard a car door slam. It didn't surprise her that Fez had heard it open when the humans hadn't. Horses had very keen hearing.

"Excuse me, but I bet that's Callie," Scott said. "I'll go check and bring her back here, okay?"

"Oh, sure," Carole said. Scott was gone instantly. That meant Callie would probably be there in a few minutes. Carole glanced around. Was the stall ready for Callie's inspection? Ben had been so busy with his grooming that he hadn't noticed that Fez had eaten some of the hay in the tick. What if Callie thought they hadn't given him enough food? And the water? There was work to be done.

Callie stepped back from her father's car. "I'll see you tonight," she said through the open car window.

"Bye, honey," the congressman answered. "Remember to be home on time. Your mother has promised to make everybody's favorite dinner."

"Oh, right, that pizza place that delivers—"

"Full pepperoni, half mushroom," he said.

"Hope they're as good as the place back home."

"They are," he said. "You'll see."

Callie waved, and her father pulled out of the drive.

She paused to look around. The place didn't look like much, but then stables usually didn't win awards for architecture. There was a single large house, probably where the owner lived. Max something. Regnery—she remembered. He'd had a couple of pretty good riders come through his school. Dorothy DeSoto, who had been big about ten years earlier, had trained here. He had a good reputation. Not that he was known for endurance riding, but he was good with horses and riders. That was all that mattered to Callie. She had her own trainer. Or at least she used to have her own trainer. Back home.

It was the second time in as many minutes that the phrase had gone through her head. Home was a long way away, on the other side of the country. But her father's work was here now most of the year. Some congressmen left their families "back home." For her father, that wouldn't do. He wanted them to be together. So Scott and Callie had finished out the school year at their high school "back home" and had come to join their parents. They'd go to school here next year. She'd finish high school in Virginia, apply to college from Virginia, call Virginia home. No, she couldn't do that. Home was back there, on the West Coast, where she came from, where she belonged.

She wasn't ever going to belong here. She wasn't ever going to like people, make friends, understand that soft Southern accent so many people had. Her friends were going to be on the other end of a long-distance call or on e-mail. She'd ride this horse. She'd earn ribbons, maybe even a few blues. But staying in a house in Virginia wasn't the same thing as living there. As far as Callie was concerned, "back home" was still home.

The screen door of the stable swung open and slammed shut.

It was Scott. She'd seen the car, so she knew he was there. Typical of him to have found his way into the barn. He'd probably already made friends with everyone. Scott was a natural-born friend to everyone. It was a skill he had clearly picked up from their father. He was funny, warm, kind, attentive, amusing, and comfortable with everyone. The worst part was that he actually meant it, too—at least when it came to everyone else. When he came to his sister, he wasn't always Mr. Smooth.

"Where have you been?" he demanded.

"I was waiting for Dad," Callie said. "I couldn't leave without him."

"Well, I may leave here without you," he said. "I've got an appointment with the coach of the debate team in exactly fifteen minutes, and I have to get you to the dentist first. You've got to get in there, check out your horse, who looks just fine if you want my opinion, and then we've got to get out of here in five minutes so I can take you to your appointment."

"Five minutes? Scott, I can't do that! This is the first time I've seen the horse in months. I can't just wave to him. You don't know the first thing about—"

"What I know is that I don't have a lot of time. Make it snappy."

"I'll do my best." She sighed. Scott wasn't improving her mood.

"Inside, turn right down the aisle. He's in the last stall on the right. There's a girl named Carole and a boy named Ben looking after him, but I think the horse is in a really bad mood. I guess they had to go to a lot of trouble to get him off the van—not that he got hurt or anything. I'll be waiting in the car."

"Thanks," she said.

She stepped into the stable and paused for a moment. She heard Scott turn on the motor. It irritated her. She knew it was his way of reminding her, as if she hadn't gotten the message, that he really was in a hurry. She knew he was rushed, just as she knew that he hadn't been thrilled with his assignment to pick her up and drive her around. He wasn't a lot happier about moving to Willow Creek than she was, and the only thing that made it easier for him was the excellent reputation of the Willow Creek High School debate team, a reputation he fully expected to help improve.

It took a few seconds for her eyes to adjust to the darkness after the bright summer sun outside. The stable was clean, with just the right amount of disarray. The pitchfork was precisely (and safely) tucked in a corner, but three lead ropes hung loosely around a peg, available on a second's notice. Just as they should be.

She peered into the tack room. Tack rooms always looked messy to the untrained eye. Callie's eye wasn't untrained. She could see that everything in there had a place where it belonged. The pungent smells of leather, horses, and saddle soap combined comfortably.

She'd never been to Pine Hollow before, but she knew the place. It had all the best qualities of every fine stable she'd ever walked in. This would be okay, even if it wasn't back home.

There was a long row of stalls on each side of the aisle before the right turn Scott had alerted her to. Every stall held a horse. Every stall was clean, all the horses were groomed, each of the hay ticks had a good supply of hay, and all the water buckets were filled. Pine Hollow had an excellent reputation for horse care, and Callie wasn't surprised to find everything in order. She was pleased to have the reputation confirmed, even if she could only make the judgment based on a quick peek. Once again, she found herself more than a little annoyed with her brother and his rush to deliver her to the dentist an hour before she needed to be there so he could spend extra time with the debate coach. Why was it that his appointment with the debate coach was more important than her appointment with her horse?

She hurried on along the aisle and turned right.

"Oh, hi. Where's Scott? You must be Callie."

Callie looked up to see an African American girl about her own age. The girl wore her black hair in several braids that hung down to her shoulders. She was dressed in riding jeans, stable boots, and a T-shirt. Her hair was full of straw, and there was a large splash of water down the front of her shirt. She brushed ineffectively at the straw and water.

"Right, I'm Callie," Callie confirmed testily. "And you are?"

"Oh, well, I'm Carole. Um, Carole Hanson," the girl said. "I'm in charge of the office in the mornings this summer, so I guess we'll be seeing a lot of one another, and you'll have to be sure to let me know if there are things I can do for you because we want you to be happy with Pine Hollow. It's a wonderful stable. I've been riding here since I was—oh, I guess about ten or something, and you're just going to love it here, Carrie—um, Callie."

Carole couldn't believe what she was saying, but there didn't seem to be any way to stop herself. Her mouth kept going when it was more than apparent that her brain had stopped working eight or ten sentences before. And even while those thoughts were crowding into her mind, she was still talking, by now onto the subject of feeding schedules. "And everyone pitches in. We all help around here. Of course, I do because I work here, but even when I was just a rider with her own horse here—you passed right by Starlight's—"

"Where's Fez?" Callie asked.

62

That stopped Carole. How could she be so dumb? Callie didn't need anyone to give her a sales pitch on Pine Hollow. Of course the only thing she cared about was her horse.

"Um, right here," Carole said. She took a few steps back and revealed the Arab to his new owner. "We even had his nameplate installed."

"Right," Callie said brusquely. She stepped up to the horse and took a critical look at him. "He seems to have come through the trip okay. Did he give you much trouble getting off the van?"

Carole was about to answer when she realized the question hadn't been directed to her. Callie was speaking to Ben.

"Yup," he said. He didn't elaborate. Carole envied his restraint.

Callie reached up and patted the horse. His first instinct was to pull back, but he had second thoughts about that and let her touch him. She clicked her tongue and scratched him on the cheek. He responded with as much affection as Carole had seen from him since he'd arrived.

"You're good," Carole said, genuinely admiring Callie's skill.

"I love horses, it's that simple," Callie said.

That smarted. Callie had managed to imply that Carole didn't love horses, and nothing could be farther from the truth. But Callie was a customer, a paying boarder, a congressman's daughter, a champion rider. And Carole was in charge of making her feel welcome at Pine Hollow.

"It shows," Carole told Callie. What she didn't say was that other things showed, too.

FIVE

Carole pasted a smile on her face. "I'd like to show you the office and let you see how we keep our records," she said.

"On computer, I presume," said Callie. "I don't really need to see it. I'm sure it's just fine. That's the way Henry did everything at the stable back home. It's all standard. I'm sure you're up to date."

Carole swallowed. In fact, Max had long considered shifting Pine Hollow's records to computer, but he believed that the books had the advantage of being very portable and entirely secure from the dangers of power outages. Perhaps Callie would be interested to know about that.

"Actually, we keep notebooks for each horse. That way, if there's a problem with the power, or whatever—well, you know."

"Right, whatever," Callie said, dismissing Carole and her explanation. She seemed annoyed and harried. Carole lost every bit of self-confidence she'd ever had and became convinced that Callie's annoyance was completely her fault. Normally, when the subject was horses, Carole was relaxed and at ease. Today she felt like a bundle of nerves.

Callie swallowed hard. This wasn't easy on her. Everything, including the horse she was expected to ride, was new. New wasn't something that Callie liked or did well with. She liked things that were familiar. For the umpteenth time, she found herself wishing she were as flexible as Scott. Scott was always instantly at home wherever he was—except now, of course. Right now he was out in the car, drumming his fingers on the steering wheel, waiting for Callie and wishing he could already be at the high school talking with the debate coach.

Well, Callie still had a few minutes, and she intended to use them to find out all she could about Pine Hollow and her new horse's care.

"What about the exercise schedule for boarders?" Callie asked. At her last stable, Henry had set aside Monday and Wednesday mornings and Friday late afternoons exclusively for horse owners. There were no classes at those times, so the owners could use all the facilities without competing with classes and occasional riders. It had worked well for Greensprings Stable, and she wondered if Pine Hollow had anything like it.

The question confused Carole. Boarders were

expected to exercise their own horses, and they could do it whenever they wanted. It helped if they let the office know when they were coming, but they were certainly entitled to come over anytime at all. But maybe that wasn't what Callie meant. She was, after all, a champion rider *and* the daughter of a congressman, so she was probably used to getting VIP treatment. There was no way Pine Hollow was going to come in second to any other stable.

"We'll see to it that Fez gets all the exercise he needs," said Carole.

"You turn the horses out on some sort of schedule?"

"Well, that, of course," Carole said. "But every horse has individual needs, and we'll see that they're met. A champ like Fez needs to be ridden to stay in top form."

"At least four times a week," said Callie.

"Just what I thought," said Carole. "We'll see to it as part of his board here."

"You'll do the exercising?" Callie asked.

"Well, me or whoever is available," Carole said. "Nothing but the best for our clients—and their owners."

"Oh, that's interesting," said Callie. "Back home, I always had to exercise my horse myself, and four times a week is a lot, especially when school's open. But if you can do the exercising for me—well, that takes off a lot of pressure. It'll mean that when I do ride him, I can focus on skills and not just on seeing to it that he's getting enough exercise to stay supple and strong. That's great news."

Perhaps it was great news for Callie, but Carole didn't think it was such good news for herself. She'd blundered into making an outrageously generous offer, and Callie had taken her up on it. If she'd heard herself right, she'd just told Callie she would ride Fez for at least an hour four times a week. Carole caught Ben looking at her darkly.

"Ben?" she said, hoping for some kind of rescue.

She got no rescue from him. He just nodded.

"Fez is a spirited horse," Callie began.

"I know that," said Carole.

"He's going to need a good workout every time he's ridden."

"Yes, I know."

"I always take my horse through a set of exercises, really a program, designed to work on various skills and to maintain all his body strength, because when we compete, we'll need it all—both his strength and mine. Fez'll need to be worked hard, but not exhausted. You can't wear him out; you need to strengthen him."

"I know," said Carole.

"A horse that's worked too hard before a competition doesn't have anything to give when it counts."

"Of course," said Carole.

"So it's very important that you follow a rigorous schedule. That's what I've always done in the past. I knew exactly what my last horse needed. In the case of Fez, well, it's a whole new horse with new needs. I can't take the time now to give you a program—but maybe you have some ideas."

"Sure," said Carole. By now she was feeling totally lost. She'd committed her afternoons to Fez. Why not add her evenings, too? She could develop an exercise program for this horse, couldn't she?

Callie edged toward the door. Carole was more than a little relieved to see that she was leaving. She was afraid if Callie stayed another minute, she'd make another offer Callie couldn't refuse. Perhaps their new house needed some rugs, in which case Carole was sure to offer to lie down and let the whole family walk on her!

"Look, I'll call in a couple of days and we can talk about the program you've got planned. I'll need to check it."

"Definitely," Carole said.

"Bye." Callie gave Carole and Ben an ever so slight wave of her hand and hurried out of the stable.

Carole was stunned. She still could hardly believe what had happened, what she'd said, what she'd promised. She turned to Ben for comfort. For a long moment they didn't say anything to one another. Then Ben spoke.

"Sounds like you're going to be busy this summer, Carole."

He was right about that. She'd just made a deal to exercise another owner's horse. This wasn't a service Pine Hollow normally provided, and even if it did, it wasn't something Carole was being paid to do. That meant that she was going to be doing it on her own time, and for no money. Worse still, every afternoon she spent riding Fez was an afternoon she couldn't be riding Starlight.

SIX

"Lisa! I got it!" Stevie whispered gleefully as she emerged from the manager's office. "I got a job! I'm going to make money. I'll be rich, rich, rich!"

"You mean you'll be able to pay for your insurance, insurance, insurance," Lisa teased.

"Well, that, and maybe a little bit more. People give tips, you know."

"For good service," Lisa said.

"You're being the voice of reason, and I'm not at all sure I like that."

"I'll try to do better," Lisa said. She stood up and threw her trash in the can. The two of them headed for the door. "When do you start?"

"Tonight—five o'clock sharp," Stevie said. She reached for the door.

The manager hurried out of his office. "Oh, Stephanie, I forgot to give you this," he said. He handed her a package. "It's your uniform."

"Uniform?"

"Well, really, just a hat and a T-shirt. You can wear your own jeans or skirt—whatever you want. But when you're knocking on strangers' doors, you must have something to identify yourself as the delivery person from Pizza Manor."

"Sure," Stevie said. She opened the package. The T-shirt was simple enough. It had the store's logo, a cartoon character dressed as a medieval knight. That was why it was called Pizza Manor. The hat, however, was not so simple. It was like the one the little cartoon character wore. It was made of felt, with a brim that was rolled up along the edges but pointed in front—like something Robin Hood might have worn on a bad hair day. Worst of all, feathers sprouted from the headband.

"Isn't it cute?" the manager asked.

"Very," Stevie said, hoping she was keeping her voice even. She didn't want him to sense her rising panic.

"See you later!" he said cheerfully. He retreated to his office before Stevie could reply. She turned to Polly Giacomin, who was still standing patiently behind the counter.

"Nobody told me about this!" Stevie exploded.

"Didn't you wonder why he was so worried about having to make the deliveries himself tonight?" she teased.

Lisa began giggling. "Put it on," she said.

Stevie donned the hat and slipped the elastic band under her chin. She grimaced.

Lisa adjusted the hat to a jaunty angle. "It's you!" she declared. Polly grinned.

"It's a good thing there aren't any mirrors in this place," Stevie said. "I have a feeling I'm better off not knowing how I look. Now, Polly, tell me—are there any other nasty surprises in store for me?"

"No," Polly said. "We make good pizza, so people are usually happy to have it. And they do give good tips, so all of our delivery people in the past have been pleased with that—Oh, there is one thing."

"Uh-oh," said Stevie.

"Not that bad, but I just ought to warn you. Mr. Andrews is a really nice guy, but he's totally gung ho about this place—like it's his life. He's always worried that one of us is going to do something to upset a customer. That's when he tells us to 'Mind your Pizza Manors.'"

"I'm not sure I need insurance this badly," Stevie said.

"Oh, yes you do," Lisa said.

"You're just afraid Alex will have to pay all of it," Stevie accused her.

"No. I'm just afraid you're going to want to borrow money from me and Carole," Lisa said. "Well, we're both broke, so you are going to have to wear a dumb hat and earn it. Or let Alex have the car all the time, which might be okay, too. Come on. I have to get home. Say good-bye to Polly, um, politely," she said.

Stevie turned to Polly, slid the silly hat off her head with her right hand, brandished it gallantly, then placed it over her heart while she bowed, her left foot in front of her right one. "Milady," she said.

"And you haven't even taken the training course yet!" Polly said.

Lisa hurried Stevie out of the shop before she could ask Polly what she meant. Stevie did need the job, and Lisa didn't want her to quit before she even started. Moreover, she was now crunched for time. They had to get going. She settled into the passenger seat of Stevie's car.

"Where to?" Stevie asked. "Your place or mine?"

"Mine," Lisa told her. "I've got to do some organizing for my trip, and life is easier if I do that kind of thing when Mom isn't around. Although it's been more than a year since Dad got remarried, Mom still resents it and the fact that he moved across the country. She calls Dad's new wife 'that woman,' and she won't even mention the baby. I guess I can understand. It wouldn't make me happy if I were her, but it sure has made him happy."

"It doesn't make me or Carole or Alex happy, either," Stevie said, just to remind Lisa that her mother wasn't the only one who would miss her that summer.

"It changes everything. I know that," Lisa said. "Change can be great, but sometimes it's just too much. When my parents split up and Dad moved to California, I felt like I was being cut in half—half of me loved Mom and the other half loved Dad, and the half that loved Mom hated Dad and the half that loved Dad hated Mom. It's tough having all that love and hate all mixed up inside. I mean . . . I still wish it hadn't happened, but the fact is that there was so much tension in our house all the time that life is a lot easier with them apart from one another. The real trouble is that Mom is miserable and Dad is deliriously happy. When I spend time with Mom, I try to make her feel better, and when I spend time with Dad, I'm relieved that I don't have to cope with that, and then I feel guilty that I'm relieved. Isn't that great? No matter what I do, it hurts. I feel like I'm caught in the middle. I know that how I'm feeling isn't particularly rational. I mean, none of this is my fault. But it still hurts. But as time goes by, I feel it a little bit less and hurt a little bit less. I think it's the same for Mom and Dad, too. Mom is getting better, slowly. Dad is admitting that what he did was hurtful—even if it wasn't wrong for him. And we're all going on with our lives."

Stevie was glad she was behind the wheel and could pretend she was concentrating on the road in front of her. This was the first time in more than two years that Lisa had talked so much about her parents and how their divorce had affected her. Both Stevie and Carole had known that all these things were going on in Lisa's mind and heart because they were best friends, but Lisa had never shown much inclination to talk about them. Now she was talking, and Stevie's sole job was to listen.

"So now I'm going off to my dad's. It'll be more relaxed than here—if you don't count looking after Lily. She's the cutest thing. I never thought I'd have a baby sister, and I certainly never thought it would happen when I was in high school—in a way, that's an awful thought— but it's happened and she's adorable and I love her and I'm glad to spend time with her and I'm glad to be with my dad when he's so obviously happy to have me and Evelyn and Lily there with him. It's like there's enough air out there to breathe, and there isn't here, certainly not at my house, anyway. Do you think the air in California is really different?"

"I've never been there," Stevie said. "I guess the weather's better."

"I don't think that's it," said Lisa.

"Probably not," Stevie agreed. She pulled into Lisa's driveway and stopped the car smoothly. She didn't know what to say. Everything seemed inadequate. Lisa smiled understandingly.

"Tell Alex I'm home, will you?" she asked.

"I think he knows already," Stevie said. She pointed to her own home, a few houses down the block. Alex had emerged from the front door and was heading toward Lisa's house. "Radar," Stevie said in explanation.

"Thanks," said Lisa. "For the lift and for letting me talk."

"You're welcome," Stevie said, meaning it.

"And congratulations on getting your job. Don't worry about the hat. It looks so silly on your head that nobody will take it seriously at all."

"You really know how to make a girl feel good, don't you?"

"That's what friends are for," Lisa said before she closed the car door and headed into her house.

Stevie waved at her twin as she passed him on her way back to their house. He was so focused on getting to Lisa's that Stevie didn't think he really saw her at all. That was okay. She was glad that her best friend had someone who loved her that much—even if it was only Stevie's brother.

"Hi, Lis'," Alex said, giving her a quick kiss on the cheek and taking her hand. "Got a minute?"

"Always," Lisa said, squeezing his hand back. "I wanted to see you today anyway. I've got a bunch of stuff to do, and you can help."

"Like choose what shirts you're going to take to California?"

"No, actually, what CDs I should take. That's more up your alley than fashion, right?"

"Definitely," he agreed. She led him into the den, where she kept her music collection.

As they walked in, Lisa's mother came out, saying she was on her way to the grocery store. "Not that I'm going to need to keep much food in the house once you're gone for the summer, Lisa," she said. The sigh was apparent, even though inaudible.

"That makes it unanimous, then," Alex said when the door closed behind Mrs. Atwood. "Nobody wants you to go away this summer."

"That doesn't change the fact that I'm going, Alex, and it doesn't make it easier when you talk like that."

"I know, I know. I just can't help myself sometimes."

"Look, we'll talk on the phone. I'll send you e-mail from my dad's computer. I'll be in your hair so much you'll start wishing I were farther away!"

"I don't think that'll happen," he said. Gently he pulled her to him and wrapped her in his strong arms. He gave her the kiss he'd wanted to give her when he first saw her: warm, lingering, and deep. She circled her arms around his neck and kissed him back. It made her feel good—very good—but it also reminded her how hard it was going to be to be away from him for the whole summer.

They came up for air. "I'm going to miss you," he said.

"Me too. But being apart isn't going to change how we feel about one another. Besides, Alex, saying good-bye is really hard. I'm dreading it, and it doesn't help when you start doing it now. I'm not leaving yet. Let's save the good-byes until the last minute, okay?"

Alex looked at her, savoring her sweet smile and lovely face. "I hadn't thought of it that way, but, as usual, you are totally sensible and absolutely right. No good-byes. Just hellos. I do a good hello kiss, too. Want to try it?"

"Silly!" she said, pushing him away. "You're as incorrigible as your sister! Who—by the way—got herself a job today."

"Ah, my sister the pizza girl, huh? I've heard

that Mr. Andrews is something else. The two of them should get along just fine."

"As long as she 'minds her Pizza Manors,' " Lisa said.

"You're kidding!"

Lisa told him all about Stevie's interview, including the hat. It was a useful way to change the mood because the image of Stevie in the feathered hat was so hilarious.

"And I guess she won't be the only one with a new look this summer."

"You have to wear a uniform while you mow lawns?" Lisa asked.

"No, of course not," he said. "But I will be spending the summer in the great outdoors, getting a tan that will be the envy of everyone but lifeguards."

"You be sure to wear sunscreen," said Lisa.

"Don't you want me to be a bronze god?"

"Better to be pasty white than to have skin cancer."

"Maybe a little tan?"

"Maybe," she said, relenting. "Just a little. If you get too handsome, the girls will all be after you, and I don't want that!"

"I'll beat them off with a stick," Alex promised.

"That's what I like to hear," Lisa said. "Now,

here are my CDs. Which ones do you think I can't live without for the summer?"

Alex studied the CD holder and started pulling out boxes. He made three piles. "These are mine that you borrowed," he said, pointing to the first pile. "And these are yours that you should take with you."

"What's the third pile?" she asked.

"Yours that you want to lend to me for the summer," he explained with a smile.

She was about to protest when the phone rang. She walked into the living room and picked it up.

"Hey, Lisa! You're there. It's Skye. I'm on a quick break, so I don't have long to talk, but I heard you're coming out here—that's great! Listen, will I get to see you?"

"I don't have a lot of plans, like, for instance, I'm not in any television shows or anything. My schedule is pretty much open. You're the one with all the work."

"Well, not so much I can't visit with friends sometimes. And there's something else."

"What's that?" Lisa asked.

"Um . . . ," he said. "I guess it'll be better to talk about it when you get here. When'll you arrive? Want me to send a car?"

"No thanks, Skye. My dad'll meet me."

Alex peered through the doorway, looking curious. "Who are you talking to?" he whispered.

"Skye Ransom," she mouthed back.

The concern on Alex's face was immediate and obvious. She shook her head as if to dismiss his worry. She slipped her hand over the mouthpiece. "Just a friend," she added in a whisper.

Alex nodded broadly in a general display of disbelief.

"Look, you're going to be so busy it's going to be awfully hard for us to get together," Lisa said, as much for Alex's benefit as Skye's.

"Never too busy to see a friend," Skye told her.

"I'll call your service when I get to my dad's house and we can talk."

"Good idea," Skye said. "But why don't you call me at home? You've got the number, right?"

"Right," she said. "And you have my father's number in case we get crossed up."

"Of course," he said. "From the last time you were here. That was so much fun, wasn't it?"

"Yes," she said, remembering the great time they'd had when she had come to California for her father's wedding. Lisa was uncomfortable with the idea that Alex might misinterpret what Skye was saying to her, so she was revealing as little as possible about the other end of the conversation. But she was also uncomfortably aware that Alex knew perfectly well what she was doing.

"I bet you have to get back to the set now, right?"

"Well, in a minute," Skye said.

"Okay, then I'll talk to you when I get out there."

"It's a date," he said, and hung up.

Lisa cradled the phone.

"Are you making plans with Skye?" Alex asked.

"Not likely," Lisa said. "He's so busy with his career that he hardly has any time for a life. But, Alex, even if I do see him, remember, or try to remember, that he's a friend. He's been a friend for a long time. He's never been any more than a friend, or any less. You're number one on my list, and that's not going to change."

"But you're so beautiful," Alex said. "And he's not blind."

Lisa blushed. "I suppose that means you want another kiss," she teased.

"No, it means I *really* want to borrow the Zero Gravity CD for the summer."

"But that's my favorite!" she protested.

"All the better to remember you by while you're gone," he said.

Lisa smiled and gave in. Love was complicated.

SEVEN

S tevie checked over her shoulder. In the backseat of the car was a large insulated container.
Each container could hold two pizzas. On the
front seat, next to her hat, was the list of ad-
dresses, in order, where she was to deliver the
pizzas. It wasn't actually a very long list. There
was just one address left.

Delivering pizzas was just about as routine as
Stevie had thought it would be. She delivered the
pizza, she took the money, she thanked the customer for the tip, she took off her hat and gave
her courtly bow, she waited for the inevitable
giggle, and then she left. Sometimes the door
closed before she bowed, sometimes not. She
didn't have much time to think about that. People expected pizzas to be delivered quickly,
whether they were being reasonable or not. Pizzas
that were late were also cold, which meant the
customer wouldn't be happy, meant they
wouldn't tip, meant there wasn't anything funny

or not that she could do with her silly hat that would change that. She had a job to do.

She backed the car down the Applethwaites' driveway. There was a bump, and then the left rear of the car dropped an unnerving number of inches. Stevie opened her door and looked behind her. The Applethwaites had a little flower garden bordering their concrete driveway. It now had about eight inches less of impatiens than it had had a minute earlier. She closed her door, pulled the car forward, adjusted the wheel, and backed out without inflicting further damage on the pink and white flowers. She had a brief conversation with her conscience about the damage she'd caused. She had two more pizzas to deliver right away. The Applethwaites had only tipped her a quarter, and a quick examination of the flower bed confirmed that she was hardly the first person to make that mistake. She didn't feel wonderful about her decision, but she decided to go away without saying anything.

At the next house, she banged into a garbage can and knocked it over as she came into the driveway. It was a rubber one, so it didn't make a lot of noise, and it was tightly closed, so nothing happened. Stevie righted the thing before she even rang the bell, wondering all the while why the Singers had put their garbage can right in the middle of their driveway. It belonged by the curb.

The Singers were very grateful for their pizza—two dollars more grateful than the Applethwaites. Stevie was glad she'd put the garbage can back and hoped they would want to order pizza a lot when she was on duty. She made a note to be on the lookout for their garbage can next time.

This wasn't complicated, but it was hard work—harder than she'd thought it would be, anyway. She was always rushed, and she wanted to appear unrushed. Mr. Andrews said people liked fast service, not hurried service.

Stevie returned to the shop for her next set of pizzas. This time there was only one waiting for her. She checked the slip and the order. She'd already learned that sometimes they got mixed up, and if she delivered anchovies to a sausage household, nobody would be happy. This one was right. It was a large pepperoni with mushrooms on half, and it was going to someone named Forester.

Stevie checked the address. It wasn't too far from her house. She knew the place, but she didn't remember anyone named Forester there. She was getting a vague image of the kids in the family as she drove to the house. It was a big one, nicely kept, but she was sure the family wasn't Forester.

The outside of the house was well lit. There was a two-car garage, but a vehicle was parked sideways in a turnaround part of the driveway. Beside the garage, there was a large stack of cardboard boxes. Moving cartons. Obviously, the family Stevie remembered had moved out. And now the Foresters lived there. Well, whoever they were, Stevie hoped they were big tippers.

She got out of the car, put on her silly hat, took the Foresters' pizza—still toasty warm—out of the container, and rang the doorbell.

As soon as the door began to open, Stevie spoke.

"Pizza Manor at your service, milord," she said, just as she'd been instructed.

"You've got to be kidding," said the boy who held the door.

Stevie found herself gazing into the very blue eyes of one of the best-looking guys she'd ever seen.

"I wish I were kidding," she said. "But right there in my employees manual, it says I have to say that stuff. Wait till you see what I do as I leave!"

"Well, don't hurry the process on my account," the boy said. "I'm enjoying your company."

Stevie was quite aware of the carton she was holding. The heat from the pizza had penetrated the cardboard and was doing the same to the palm of her hand. She was less than comfortable.

"Perhaps milord would like his pizza?" she asked, trying not to sound pained. " 'Twould be fully of pepperonius and a moiety of fungal deliciosity. Surely such victuals are sufficient to please the palates of the gourmettiest consumer in all the realm."

"Who can resist that?" the boy asked, and took the pizza from Stevie's hands. She blew on her palm to cool it.

"Oh, I'm sorry," the boy said. "I didn't realize the pizza would be that hot when it arrived." He turned and spoke to someone else in the hallway. "Callie, can you bring an ice cube and a piece of paper towel for our delivery person?"

"Sure," said a girl's voice.

"You've just moved in?" Stevie asked.

"Yup," said the boy. "My name's Scott Forester, and this is my sister, Callie."

Callie handed Stevie the ice cube and paper towel. Stevie thanked her and introduced herself, explaining that she lived just a few blocks away. By the time Scott had the money for Stevie—with a nice tip—they'd established that they were neighbors and that Willow Creek was a nice place to live. Scott took the pizza into the kitchen. Callie stood and chatted with Stevie for a few minutes.

"I like your earrings," Callie said. Stevie's hand flew up to her ear—she couldn't remember which pair she'd put on that morning. She shouldn't have had to check. It was her horseshoes. What other earrings would she have chosen on the day she was going to apply for both her driver's license and a job?

"Are you a rider?" Callie asked.

"As much as possible," said Stevie. "And you?"

"Definitely. I ride endurance. But we've just moved here, so I haven't tried out your trails and competition."

"Do you have a horse?"

"We're leasing a horse for the summer, with an option to buy. In fact, he just got here today. I'm boarding him at Pine Hollow. Do you know the place?"

"Every inch of it," Stevie said. "And I can tell you, you've just made the best decision of your life."

"Well, I'm glad to hear that," said Callie. "It seemed a little—"

"That's where I keep Belle—she's my horse—and my friends ride there, too. We're probably going to be seeing a lot of each other. I promise you that the next time you see me, I won't be wearing this silly hat or shirt—that is, unless you order another pizza tonight. But I spend all the time I can at Pine Hollow. Max is great. So are Red and Ben. They're the stable hands, but you probably haven't met them yet."

"Brooding kind of guy."

"That's Ben," Stevie said. "He's wonderful with horses. And my two best friends ride there, too. You're going to love them. We tried endurance riding once. But just the once. We learned a lot, but I bet you could teach us a lot more."

"Well, if you're interested—"

"I am," Stevie assured her. "Say, my friends and I are planning a trail ride in a couple of days. Would you like to come along? We'd be glad to show you the woods around here. We know just about all the trails and the nice places to stop, and where we can canter, and some fallen logs to jump—you know, that kind of thing."

"Well, are you sure it would be okay with your friends?" Callie asked.

"Absolutely," Stevie said. "We love to show off the place to newcomers."

"Well, then, I'll be there."

"Day after tomorrow," Stevie said. "We'll take off about ten, so we'll get to Pine Hollow about nine."

"See you then, if not before," Callie said. "And, uh, thanks."

"You're welcome," Stevie said. And then, just the perfect way she was supposed to, she held her hat to her chest and bowed.

"Enjoy thy pizza," she said. Callie laughed and closed the door.

PINE HOLLOW

Dear *Pine Hollow* Reader,

We want to know what you think! Please take the time to answer the following questions *after* you have read the book.
Be completely honest—there are no right or wrong answers. You don't even need a stamp; just fill out the card and drop it in the mailbox. Thanks!

1. Did you like the book? (Check one) ☐ I loved it ☐ I liked it ☐ It was OK ☐ I didn't like it ☐ I hated it

2. Would you read another *Pine Hollow* book? (Check one) ☐ Definitely Yes ☐ Probably Yes ☐ Maybe ☐ Probably Not ☐ Definitely Not

3. How did you find out about this book? (Check one) ☐ *Horse Play* magazine ☐ *Young Rider* magazine ☐ *Girl's Life* magazine ☐ Received postcard
☐ Found it in the bookstore ☐ Read about it in *Love Stories* ☐ Read about it in *The Saddle Club*

4. Please rank the following in order of importance to you in deciding to buy this book (1 being most important, 8 being least): ____ Subject/content ____ Cover
____ Friend recommended it ____ Back of book ad ____ Postcard ____ Advertisement ____ Fan of *The Saddle Club* ____ Read other horse series books

5. Would you recommend *Pine Hollow* to a friend? ☐ Definitely Yes ☐ Probably Yes ☐ Maybe ☐ Probably Not ☐ Definitely Not

6. Where did you get this book? ☐ Walden ☐ Borders ☐ Barnes & Noble ☐ Equestrian store (Store name)_____
☐ Other bookstore ☐ Discount store (like K-Mart) ☐ Grocery store ☐ Received as a gift ☐ Other (Please specify)_____

7. Who chose this book? (Check one) ☐ I did ☐ Friend ☐ Parent/Grandparent ☐ Other (Please specify)_____

8. Who paid for this book? (Check one) ☐ I did ☐ Friend ☐ Parent/Grandparent ☐ Other (Please specify)_____

9. Which of these books/series have you read? (Check all that apply) ☐ The Saddle Club ☐ Thoroughbred ☐ Pony Tails ☐ Pony Camp ☐ Riding Academy

10. Do you ride horseback? Yes No (Circle one) If yes, how many times did you ride last month? ☐ 1-2 ☐ 3-4 ☐ 5+

11. On a scale of 1-10 (1 is worst, 10 is best) how does *Pine Hollow* rank as a series?____

12. Which, if any, of these magazines do you read regularly? (Check all that apply) ☐ *Horse Illustrated* ☐ *Horse Play* ☐ *Young Rider* ☐ *Teen People*
☐ *Sports Illustrated for Kids* ☐ *Teen* ☐ *Seventeen* ☐ *Jump!* ☐ *YM* ☐ *Girls' Life* ☐ Other (Please specify)_____

Your Name_____ Date of Birth____/____/____

Address_____ City_____ State_____ Zip_____

BUSINESS REPLY MAIL

FIRST-CLASS MAIL   PERMIT NO. 01239   NEW YORK, NY

POSTAGE WILL BE PAID BY ADDRESSEE

BANTAM DOUBLEDAY DELL
BOOKS FOR YOUNG READERS
MARKETING DEPT.
1540 Broadway
New York NY 10109–1225

Stevie felt wonderful. She'd met two nice people, one of them a rider who already had a horse at Pine Hollow. What a great day this was turning out to be—if you didn't count some mushed impatiens, and Stevie didn't.

Stevie slid behind the wheel of her car and plopped her silly hat on the seat. That was when she noticed that her beeper was going off. Mr. Andrews had given it to her so that he could let her know when she had to hurry back to the shop. She'd been so happy about chatting with the Foresters that she'd almost forgotten she actually had a job to do. She'd taken a long time to deliver just one pizza.

She fastened her seat belt, turned the key, and shifted into reverse. She checked the mirror and began backing down the driveway carefully. There was a flower bed on the left side and the parked car on her right.

"What is it about impatiens?" Stevie asked her rearview mirror. "Why does everybody in this town have a border of impatiens next to their driveway? Is this a test?"

She checked over her left shoulder and then looked back into the mirror. The flower bed was safe this time. Cautiously she proceeded.

There was an unfamiliar feeling that Stevie didn't like at all, and she met some resistance when she put her foot on the gas pedal ever so lightly. She looked over her right shoulder. The car that was parked sideways in the turnaround area was right there. Stevie gulped, shifted into drive, and pulled ahead about a foot. She hurried out of the car, dreading what she might find.

She was right to worry. She'd broken her taillight and dented the area all around it. It was bad, really bad. She could barely bring herself to look at the other car, but she forced herself.

The other car was a Jeep. That meant it was expensive, but it also meant it was tough. Where Stevie's car had really visible damage, it wasn't so clear that the Foresters' car did. There was a scratch. And there was a slight dent—or maybe that's how the car was made. Stevie scooted over to the other side to see if it went that way, too. But it was dark outside, and the lights from the house cast dark shadows on that side of the car. She couldn't see. She really didn't know.

It wasn't like the impatiens at the Applethwaites' house. Stevie knew she'd done that and didn't really care because they'd been so stingy and because so many other people had obviously done exactly the same thing she had to the flowers.

There was a scratch on the Foresters' car, but Stevie couldn't believe she had done that. She'd been driving so slowly, how could she possibly have done any kind of damage? And *if* there was damage, there wasn't much of it. A little scratch like that could have happened anytime. Yesterday, last week, a year ago. How would anybody ever know?

Stevie heard the beeper go off again. She had to hurry or Mr. Andrews would be totally annoyed with her.

She was pretty sure she hadn't damaged the Foresters' car. The damage to her car had almost certainly bccn caused by the big protective bumper on the van. Definitely, Stevie decided.

She got back into her car and backed down the driveway very carefully. She decided that from then on, she would park at the curb and carry the pizzas up to the houses.

EIGHT

"Come on, boy," Carole said to Fez the next morning. "You're about to get your first taste of riding Pine Hollow style." She gripped the horse's reins firmly and led him out of his stall toward the schooling ring, where she was going to begin fulfilling her inexplicable promise to the congressman's daughter.

Carole had ridden many horses over the years—easy ones, tough ones, old plugs, champion hunter jumpers, and priceless racehorses. Every one of them was a new experience for her, and every new experience was a good one in its own way. She wondered how this horse was going to fit into that.

Fez followed Carole dutifully out of his stall and down the stable aisle. He was getting his first real look at his new home, and Carole didn't rush him. He had every right to be curious. He eyed all the other horses as he passed them. He showed little interest, but Carole was sure he was taking it in.

She mounted and then walked him over to the good-luck horseshoe, one of Pine Hollow's oldest traditions. Three generations before, the founder of Pine Hollow, Max Regnery, Sr., had nailed this horseshoe over the entry to the main outdoor ring. He instituted a rule for all his students that they had to touch the horseshoe before riding—every time, without fail. He told them the horseshoe had special good luck, and if they followed the rule, they wouldn't get hurt. It seemed to work. In fact, no one at Pine Hollow had ever gotten seriously injured while riding.

The little kids who rode at the stable believed deeply in the magic of the horseshoe. Carole suspected something else was at work. Touching the horseshoe was a way of reminding oneself that riding could be a dangerous sport. People could, and did, get hurt when riding, but a lot of riding accidents were the result of carelessness. Riders who remembered the dangers tended to be sensible and cautious. The horseshoe was strong preventive medicine.

Fez flinched and nearly bolted before Carole had a chance to make contact with the horseshoe.

"No way!" she said. "I know you're a handful, and there's no way I'm taking a chance. I'm going to touch that horseshoe before we take one more step."

Fez pulled at the reins and pranced nervously, but he did what he was told, and Carole managed a successful swipe at the horseshoe before she and Fez entered the schooling ring.

It was early in the morning, and she had the place to herself. The only way she could get in a brief stretch of exercise for Fez that day was to do it before work. She'd been hoping to have a chance to ride Starlight, but that would have to wait until the trail ride the next day.

Carole's plan was to give Fez an easy workout for his first full day at Pine Hollow. She wanted it to be easy for both of them, since she had a full morning ahead of her, including a whole class of young riders who needed pony assignments and a meeting with the grain salesman to go over a mysterious and complicated bill. They began at a walk, and after a few times around the ring, she gave Fez a signal to trot. He was slow to respond. A well-trained champion horse like Fez should be eager to move to a more rapid gait, but he didn't seem eager to do anything she asked of him. It took three kicks and a flick of her crop to get his attention.

It was a frustrating business. Carole wondered if her annoyance with herself was affecting the way she was riding Fez and the way he was reacting to her, but she dismissed the idea. She knew how to ride. She also knew better than to take out her frustrations on a horse.

As the ride went on, she found that she had enough frustration to take out on a hundred horses. Champion though he might be, Fez was no joy to ride. She felt as if he were giving her a fight about everything. No wonder he was an endurance champion—any rider would have to have a lot of endurance to put up with this!

Carole took a deep breath and held her temper. How could she be mad at Fez? He must be terribly confused. He'd just had a long trip, which he clearly hadn't liked. He was in a new stable, surrounded by totally new horses, handled by totally new people, probably eating a new mixture of grains, exercising in an unfamiliar schooling ring. Everything had to be frightening to him. There was no reason why his rider should be frightening, too.

Carole leaned forward and gave him an affectionate pat on his neck. "Good boy," she said. "I know you're trying, and I'll try, too. We'll do just fine together. You don't have to worry, because I'd never do anything to hurt you. I'll be gentle as can be and take good care of you."

In thanks, Fez bucked.

Fifteen frustrating minutes later, Carole began

thinking about how much fun it was going to be to assign ponies for the beginner class. That was when Stevie arrived. As far as Carole was concerned, Stevie was the proverbial knight on the white horse—only in this case, it was a good thing she arrived without a horse, because Carole was more than willing to provide one.

"Can you give me a hand here?" Carole asked.

"Sure," Stevie said. Carole wondered briefly if she should leave Stevie in blissful ignorance and abandon her to Fez. Somehow that didn't seem fair.

She rode over to where Stevie stood by the fence and dismounted. Fez relaxed instantly, and Carole was amused to see that he was clearly as relieved to have her out of his saddle as she was to be out.

"I've done something dumb and I really need some help," Carole confessed. "This is Fez. He's new at the stable and he's like a VIP. The owner was here yesterday. She was difficult, fussy, and moody, and she kept telling me how wonderful her last stable was. Well, you know how I am. I can't stand the idea that anybody thinks any other stable is better than Pine Hollow, and she gave the strong impression that her horse was exercised by the staff as part of his board there, so naturally—"

"Carole, you didn't!"

"Well, I guess I did," Carole said. "I told her I'd exercise him four days a week."

"Right, like Max is going to pay you for that?"

"Not a chance," Carole said. "I know. It's on me. I'm going to have to deal with it, and soon. But until I do, I made a promise. Now, I've got a whole bunch of stuff to do in the office before the beginners arrive. Can you give this guy the rest of his workout?"

"I'm always happy to ride," Stevie said.

"This may be an exception," said Carole. "He's a real handful—as bad as his owner. The workout is simple, though. He's just got to get some kinks out. Loosen him up until he's relaxed, maybe another half hour."

"Oh, sure," Stevie said. "You let me take care of this boy. All he needs is a little of Stevie's special tender loving care. He'll be putty in my hands in no time."

"Thanks," Carole said, handing her the reins. "But don't forget to touch the horseshoe."

Before Stevie could ask for any more information, Carole had headed for the office.

It only took a few minutes for Stevie to see what Carole was talking about. This horse was a handful. There were some horses it would be wonderful to exercise, but this guy—what was his name?—was going to take more than a little getting used to.

Walk, trot, canter. He did them all, but he balked and fussed. She didn't like to use her crop on an unfamiliar horse, but when she did, he didn't pay any more attention to her. She decided to use a gentle hand while she and the horse got used to one another. It meant generally letting him have his way, but it also meant they weren't fighting all the time, and at the very least it meant that he got the exercise he needed, even if he didn't get the discipline routine training required. Tomorrow would be another day.

When she'd finished putting him through his paces—or, more accurately, letting him put himself through whatever paces he wanted to go through—she dismounted and walked him around the ring to cool him down. They'd need to be out of the ring before the beginner class started.

The second time around the ring, she noticed that she was being watched. It was Callie, the girl she'd met last night. Stevie walked over to her.

"Welcome to Pine Hollow!" she said.

"Well, thank you," said Callie. "You're riding early this morning."

"I'm doing someone a favor," Stevie said as she dismounted. "This horse belongs to some difficult VIP who has just started here, and my friend was trying to soothe some ruffled feathers, so she offered to exercise him for the owner—"

Something was wrong, and Stevie knew it before she could stop the words from tumbling out of her mouth.

"I guess that would make me the difficult VIP with the ruffled feathers," Callie said.

"Oh, no, I'm sure there's a mistake here," Stevie said, but she knew the mistake was hers. "I probably totally misunderstood. Anyway, I've been riding this horse and he's a handful, so I guess what my friend meant was that the horse is difficult. I just wasn't listening too carefully because the horse is so, um, well, he's a beauty, but he *is* hard to handle. Didn't you say he was a new horse for you?" There had to be some way to deflect the conversation into a safer zone.

"We're renting him with an option to buy. Fez has been winning endurance ribbons all over the place. I'm sure he's feisty. I know he gave that girl—Carole?—trouble yesterday when he got off the van. But I rode him before we signed his papers and he's good—that is, if you know how to handle him."

"I guess I have some learning to do," Stevie said, still trying to recover from one of the most embarrassing situations she'd ever created. "But I'm about done with his exercise. I think he's loosened up, and he won't be so difficult tomorrow."

"I'm sure you're right," Callie said. "I have to go now—unless you need me to do something with Fez?"

"No, no, I'll take care of him," Stevie said. "I'd like the chance to get to know this champ a little better. Grooming is a good way to make friends. Um, how was the pizza?"

"The—? Oh, right, the pizza. Last night. It was fine. Thanks. Well, see you sometime."

"Tomorrow," Stevie said. "Remember the trail ride?"

"You sure? This isn't just something nice to do for a hard-to-handle VIP?"

"No, I'm sure. And it'll be good for Fez here," Stevie said. "He'll love to spend some time in the woods. It'll feel like home to him."

"Right," said Callie. "Tomorrow. Bye."

"Bye," said Stevie. She leaned against the fence and watched Callie walk back to the car that was waiting for her. Stevie thought she had never in her life been so glad to have a conversation end. She'd liked Callie from the moment she'd met her the night before, and she thought Callie liked her. This was someone she could be friends with, and any friend of Stevie's was bound to be a friend of Carole's and Lisa's. Well, that was a great way to begin a friendship! She'd insulted Callie and betrayed Carole's confidence.

Fez broke into her unhappy thoughts by nipping at her shoulder.

"I guess I deserve that," Stevie told the horse. "That and more. Think you could kick me a few times? Throw me when we go over a fence? Whatever you do, it wouldn't hurt as much as what I've done to myself, that's for sure."

Fez just stared at her silently. "All right, then I'll groom you. If I work hard enough, maybe it'll make me forget what I just said to skewer my best friend. Shall we give it a try?"

For the first time that day, Fez behaved perfectly. He followed Stevie's slightest signal to return to the stable and stood absolutely still while she groomed him.

The work wasn't enough to distract her, though. All she could think of was how much she'd been looking forward to going on the trail ride with Carole and Lisa. This would be their last trail ride together for months, until Lisa got back from California.

And now she had two little things she had to share with Carole. First she had to confess that she'd told Callie that Carole thought she was difficult, and then she had to tell Carole that she'd had the foresight to invite the aforementioned difficult rider along on their trail ride!

No, Stevie told herself. It wasn't even nine o'clock in the morning and she'd already made enough terrible mistakes for a week, much less a day. Confessing to Carole was almost certainly going to lead to at least one more mistake. That could wait.

NINE

Carole was on the phone when Stevie stuck her head into the office the next morning at quarter of nine. Stevie had arrived early so that she'd have a chance to talk to Carole and let her know she'd invited Callie along.

Stevie waved to get Carole's attention.

"No, of course we're having the class, Mrs. Van Buren," Carole said into the phone. "It's just that Max will be teaching it instead of—um, yes, he's a good instructor—Well, he owns the place. He's taught for years. He was practically born on a—Mrs. Van Buren—"

Carole's eyes rolled up to the ceiling. Obviously she was having a difficult phone conversation with somebody who *(a)* wasn't listening and *(b)* wouldn't have understood what she was hearing even if she had been listening. Carole circled her ear with her finger to indicate her feelings about Mrs. Van Buren's sanity. Stevie nodded.

Finally Carole convinced Mrs. Van Buren that

Max would be a worthy instructor for her first lesson. She cradled the phone. "The whole world has gone crazy," she told Stevie.

"Well, since we're on the subject," Stevie said, recognizing a chance to segue when she heard one. "There's something—"

Four little girls shoved past Stevie and planted themselves in front of Carole's desk.

"Erin said you said she could ride Patch today," one of them began.

"But you told me Max said the one who did the best in the relay races could have Patch this week, but Erin didn't do best, even though her team won. Sophie was the best and she doesn't want Patch, she wants to ride Penny, so Caitlin should get Patch, but she told Max I kicked Peso too hard, but that's not true, so she shouldn't be able to ride Patch—"

"Stop, stop, stop!" Carole said, putting her hands over her ears. "The pony assignments are posted in the tack room. No changes will be made. Period. Nobody's riding Patch because he's got a swollen ankle and I know you didn't kick Peso and there's only fifteen minutes until class starts so what are you doing here?"

The little girls fled.

"Uh, speaking of difficult, well, I mean, fussy riders—" Stevie began.

The phone rang. Carole answered it and then

listened intently. "No, Mr. Burns. I am sure that what we ordered was oats and not pellets. We have pellets left, so we wouldn't—" She covered the mouthpiece and looked at Stevie. "I spent half an hour with this man yesterday and today he wants to go over it all again— Uh, yes, Mr. Burns. I have a copy of the purchase order. I gave it to you yesterday. . . . Yes, sure, I'll fax you another copy, but in the meantime, Mr. Burns— Mr. Burns?" She hung up the phone. "That man is impossible!" she said.

"Well, yes, some people are," said Stevie. "Look, there's something I need to talk to you about."

"Thank heavens we'll have time to talk on the trail ride. This place is a zoo; I can't wait for the peace and quiet of the woods. Could you tack up Starlight for me?"

"Of course," Stevie said. "But before then, Carole, you should know—"

The phone rang again. "Yes, Mr. Burns. Well, I'm glad you found it. . . . No, Mr. Burns, that's not this order, you're looking at the purchase order from last month." Carole put her hand over the mouthpiece and spoke with Stevie while Mr. Burns droned on. "I'll see you in the stable as soon as I can get away from here. Okay?"

"Okay," Stevie agreed. It wasn't okay, but she

knew she couldn't do anything about it right then.

Lisa was giving Prancer a quick brushing when Stevie returned with Belle's tack. The two of them worked side by side, chatting about the commotion around them while they tacked up their horses.

"Morning, Stevie," Callie Forester said.

"Oh, hi, Callie. I want you to meet Lisa Atwood, one of my best friends. Lisa, I didn't have a chance to tell you yet, but I invited Callie to come along on our trail ride. She's new to Willow Creek as well as to Pine Hollow, so I thought this would be a good chance to show off the place." She quickly explained how she'd met Callie when she'd delivered pizza to her house.

Lisa smiled warmly at Callie, but the glance she gave Stevie was quizzical. Stevie knew she deserved it. This was supposed to be a trail ride for three old friends, not for newcomers, even nice newcomers.

"Welcome to Pine Hollow, Callie," Lisa said. "Is that pretty Arab down the hallway yours?"

"Yep, that's right. And this will be the first chance I've had to ride him here. I'm really looking forward to it."

"Callie does endurance riding," Stevie said. "I mean, she's really good. She's won all sorts of junior competitions."

"Not here," Callie said. "Back home."

"Where's home?" Lisa asked.

"Out on the West Coast. We just moved here. Well, my dad's been here since January. He's a congressman, and he just got elected. So we'll be here at least two years—just long enough to get me and my brother through high school. He'll be a senior, and I'm going into my junior year. It was really tough moving."

"I can relate to that," said Lisa. "Not that I've moved, exactly, but my parents got a divorce and my dad's remarried and he's living in California—"

"Where?"

"Near Los Angeles. And I'm going there for the summer—"

"It's so hard!" said Callie. "Maybe even harder for you because it's not permanent. It's just for a couple of months, and without going to school, it's almost impossible to get to know people."

"Thanks for reminding me," Lisa said sardonically.

"I'm sorry. I just meant I understand."

Lisa smiled. "I know that's what you meant. Did you live near Los Angeles?"

"No, we were up north, in a little town. I could do a lot of riding there."

"That's one thing your little town and Willow Creek have in common. You can do a lot of riding here. The school is close enough that you can actually come over every day after school if you want. Before, too."

"You can count on me being here," said Callie. "Even though the stable said they'd exercise Fez for me, I'd like to do it myself most of the time."

"Max'll ride him for you?" Lisa asked. That didn't sound like Max at all. In the first place, he didn't have time, and in the second place, he thought it was really important for the owners to ride their horses. Otherwise, why did they have them?

"No, it wasn't Max. It was that girl—I keep forgetting her name. She said she'd take care of it, so how could I refuse? Oh, that's her," she said, nodding at Carole, who was walking toward them.

"Hi, Carole," Lisa greeted her friend. "Did you meet Callie yet? Yeah, I guess you did. Anyway, she's coming along on our trail ride. Stevie met her the other night when she was delivering pizza to her house. Small world, huh? And, wait until you see her horse. Oh. You probably did see her horse, didn't you?"

"Callie and I have met," Carole said.

"Right after Fez arrived," Callie added.

Lisa knew an undercurrent when she was standing in the middle of one. What she didn't know was where this one had come from. Carole was upset about something, and it seemed as if it had to do with Callie, but maybe it was something that had happened in the office. "Stevie said things were wild in the office. The phone wouldn't stop ringing and the kids kept barging in. You must be glad to have an excuse to escape for a while. Is Emily here?"

"Yes, she's here," Carole said. She glanced back and forth between Stevie and Callie, recalling how Stevie seemed to have been in a rush to tell her something when everything was going crazy in the office. Of course, now she realized it was about Callie. Carole hadn't known they'd already met. And she certainly hadn't known that Callie was coming along on their special farewell ride. What could Stevie have been thinking?

Then she figured it out. Stevie had invited Callie to ride with them so that Carole wouldn't have to exercise Fez that afternoon. She was probably just trying to do the right thing, so it was hard for Carole to be angry with her, but that didn't mean Carole wanted to spend a couple of hours riding with Callie. Maybe Carole hadn't made it clear to Stevie that the human VIP was as difficult as the horse one. But that didn't make it okay, and it didn't make Carole want to be a part of it.

"Listen, something's come up."

"With that Mr. Burns?" asked Stevie.

"That and about fourteen other things. You

111

know how crazy it can get on summer mornings. It was probably a mistake to think I could go riding in the first place, but I definitely can't go with you guys now. I've got to stay here. Starlight needs a little workout, for sure, but I'm going to have to do it in the ring so that people can hassle me about pony assignments, grain orders, and manure disposal while I ride. You all go on ahead."

"But Carole—" Lisa protested.

"Don't worry. We'll have some time together later. You'll be back about noon, and I'll meet you guys at the usual place."

Without offering further explanation or waiting for protests, Carole spun around to leave her friends alone. She was angry. Very angry. And hurt. Their final trail ride of the summer was being interrupted by Callie Forester. If the girl loved "back home" so much, Carole wished she'd just go there—go anyplace, in fact, other than Pine Hollow.

What was done was done. Carole couldn't change it. She just didn't want to upset her friends, and she wasn't going to let Callie see her cry.

Stevie felt terrible. She knew she'd made a mistake. In fact, it seemed as if she was doing nothing but making mistakes these days. She'd hurt Carole's feelings and that bothered her, but it bothered her even more that she had messed up this trail ride. It was supposed to be fun. It was supposed to be great. When she'd invited Callie along, she'd been sure that both Lisa and Carole would like Callie as much as she did. How could she have known that wouldn't be so? And what had Callie done to make Carole think she was difficult? She seemed perfectly nice to Stevie.

Time would tell. And time was passing.

"Boy, it's too bad Carole can't come along," said Lisa.

"Yes," Callie agreed. "I wanted a chance to get to know her better. It was sort of rushed before."

Stevie wondered what that meant.

"Come on, let's get going," Lisa said. "If we stand still for a minute longer, Max will try to con us into helping tack up the ponies for the beginners."

"Okay," Stevie said, mounting Belle. "We're off, and Lisa and I promise to give you the grand tour of Pine Hollow. First stop, the good-luck horseshoe."

Stevie led the way out of the stable, through the paddocks, and into the woods behind Pine Hollow. Although it wasn't yet ten o'clock, the summer sun was already hot. The sweet scent of fresh field grass combined with the ever wonderful smells of horses and leather. It was a combination that never failed to make her feel better. The sun sparkled through the leaves, dappling the bridle trail. Beneath her, Stevie felt the wonderful warm power of her beloved Belle. She could feel her own worry and distress practically melt in the warm June day.

Behind her, Lisa and Callie were chatting easily.

". . . Well, the worst part of the election was when the whole family got interviewed by this local television station. Do you know how hard it is to smile for two hours? And out of that, they only ran about three minutes of the interview. Just two and a half seconds of that was about me."

"Were you smiling?"

"You bet I was!" Callie said, laughing. "I wasn't going to ruin Dad's future with a single grimace."

"It must be awful being on display all the time."

"Well, it really isn't all the time. In a way, too, it was harder out there where there's only one congressman in the district and it's Dad. Here, near Washington, there are loads of them. It seems like nobody gives it a second thought."

"People aren't impressed here until you get to be a senator," said Lisa, smiling.

"Unless you're indicted," Stevie said. "I mean,

if you can rustle up a good scandal, everybody will be wowed!"

"I think we'll try to avoid that," said Callie. "My dad's not the love nest type."

"So, you've got a great set of parents and a funny, flirty brother—wait'll you meet Scott, Lisa. It's a perfect life," said Stevie.

"Not totally," said Callie. "I mean, I don't have a car to drive because I'm still grounded for something I did back home. If I want to go anywhere I'm at the mercy of my flirty brother, who, as you may have noticed, is interested in chatting with almost anybody but me. Most of the time I'm stuck with a bicycle, and I feel like I'm too old for a bike. I envy you your car."

"It's just part-time," said Stevie. "I share it with my twin brother. Sharing has not always been our strongest quality, but we do okay on that because we agreed to a schedule. So far, it's worked out. But that may not mean much. We just got our licenses this week."

Callie laughed.

"You'll do fine on the sharing," Lisa said. "I'll see to it."

"Maybe," said Stevie. "Anyway, I love driving, and anytime I actually have the car, I'd be glad to drive you anywhere. No excuse is too slight for a good long ride—whether it's in a car or on horseback."

"Check," said Callie. "And I'm glad I've got a witness to what you just said, because I will definitely take you up on that."

"No problem," Stevie assured her. "And I already know where you live. And what you like on your pizza."

"See what happens when you're in the public eye?" Callie said to Lisa. "People keep dossiers on you. *Lifestyles of the Impoverished and Not Very Famous.* Now, where's this famous creek you kept talking about? My feet are getting hot and sweaty. They could use a good cool dunk."

"Right this way, milady," Stevie said.

Callie laughed and followed Stevie, happy and relaxed for the first time since she'd arrived in Willow Creek. She liked these girls. Fez was behaving better than he had the last time she'd ridden him, and she suspected it was because he was comfortable being sandwiched between Stevie's Belle and Prancer, the horse Lisa was riding.

Callie just wished everybody at Pine Hollow was as nice as Lisa and Stevie.

TEN

Carole slid the final updated notebook onto the shelf above her desk and stretched. She'd finished the work she'd needed to get done, and she could relax because it was noon. Denise would be at the office in a few minutes to relieve her for the day. That meant Carole could go home—or she could wait for her friends and go over to TD's for something to eat. It wouldn't be as good as a trail ride would have been, but at least it would be just the three of them. She promised herself for the umpteenth time that she wouldn't say anything to Stevie about inviting Callie along. Stevie had her reasons and that was that.

As soon as Denise arrived, Carole walked out to the schooling ring. From there, she'd be able to see her friends when they returned from their ride.

Everything at Pine Hollow seemed wonderfully normal on this hot summer day. Max was finishing up a jump class with the beginning riders. The next class was warming up their horses by walking them around the ring, waiting for Max to come teach them equitation. Nearby, Ben waited to help riders untack their horses and groom them. The riders would do all the work—or at least most of it—because that was the way it was done at Pine Hollow, but Ben would be sure it was done correctly.

"A penny for your thoughts," said a familiar voice.

Carole turned to see Emily Williams grooming her horse, PC, in the stall closest to the door.

"They're not worth that much," Carole assured her.

"I'm not so sure about that," Emily countered. "It takes more than a penny's worth of thinking to figure out why it was that you skipped the trail ride with your friends today. It wasn't because you don't trust me to look after the office."

"No, of course it wasn't," Carole said. "It's just that something came up."

"Okay," Emily said agreeably. "I don't have to know everything, but that doesn't keep me from *wanting* to know everything."

"Right," Carole said. She really didn't want to tell Emily everything that had happened. None of it felt right, and that wasn't something she wanted to share, even with a good friend. "Can I give you a hand with PC?" she offered.

"No thanks. I thought I'd take advantage of the extra free time I have to give him a first-class grooming. What I didn't know was how badly he needed it. His idea of the perfect way to celebrate the beginning of summer is to roll in the mud in the little paddock. So it's been beauty day for Prince Charming."

Carole peered at her friend. She was wearing a Pine Hollow T-shirt over her riding clothes to keep them clean. Emily supported herself with one crutch while she groomed her horse with one hand. Everything she did took her twice as much effort as it would anybody else, and she still managed to do three times as good a job.

"Pass me the rag, will you?" Emily asked. Carole stepped into the stable and handed her the towel. As Emily rubbed, PC's coat began to shine.

"I'd better go get my sunglasses," Carole said. "All that glare . . ."

"Flattery will get you nowhere," Emily said. "You're going to have to groom your own horse."

"I already did that. Now I'm just waiting for Lisa and Stevie to get back." Carole turned to look outside. Across the field, she could see some riders emerging from the woods. "And I think my wait's over. Listen, thanks for being willing to cover for me this morning, Emily, even if it turned out I didn't need you."

"Anytime, Carole," Emily said.

Carole walked to the door of the stable and climbed onto the paddock fence so that she could welcome the trail riders back. The three of them rode abreast, Callie in the middle. Callie was doing well with that handful of a horse she had. Carole didn't like to admit it, but Callie was doing much better with Fez than she had. She wished she could flatter herself by saying that Fez was easier for Callie to ride because Carole had exercised him so successfully, but she suspected there wasn't any truth to that.

Carole had to wait until the riders were within a hundred yards of the stable before any of them saw her perched on the fence.

It was Lisa, finally, who spotted her. "Hi, Carole. We missed you!"

"Terribly!" said Stevie.

"Did you show Callie everything?" Carole asked.

"Absolutely," Stevie said. "Now she and Fez know all our secrets."

Carole smiled on the outside. She knew Stevie was just joking, but it didn't feel like a joke.

Carole opened the paddock gate, and the girls rode to the stable entrance before dismounting. Carole had brought a small supply of carrots for the horses. Just riding on a trail was generally considered as much of a treat for the horses as the riders, but no excuse was too slight to give Belle and Prancer rewards for good behavior. Carole handed some treats to Callie to give to Fez as well.

"Speaking of treats," Stevie began, "did you say something about TD's?"

"I did," Carole said. "And as soon as I've groomed Fez, we can go over there."

"You don't have to groom him, Carole. I'll take care of it," said Callie. "You've already had one plan canceled this morning. You should have time for a nice long visit with Lisa and Stevie without worrying about me or my horse."

"Okay, thanks," Carole said, looking at Callie curiously. What she'd said sounded perfectly normal and straightforward, but Carole wondered if perhaps Callie just didn't trust her to groom the horse. No, that didn't seem likely. After all, she was trusting her to ride him.

Carole set her concerns aside and focused on helping Lisa and Stevie finish their chores so that they could get down to the serious matter of spending precious time together. It didn't take long. Less than an hour later, they were sliding into their usual booth at the ice cream parlor.

This had been a tradition among the friends for a long time—as long as they'd known one another. It was always TD's, it was always the

121

same booth, it was almost always the same waitress. Every once in a while, they'd find someone else in "their" booth. They all swore the food didn't taste as good if they ate it at another table.

Stevie picked up a menu. "This should be something special," she said. "We won't be doing it again for a long time."

"Don't remind me," Lisa said. "I've already lectured your brother about not beginning to say good-bye before we absolutely have to."

"Okay, okay," Stevie agreed. "So I'll pretend I'm not sorry you're going away. But I'm still going to have something special. What I mean by that is something that isn't pizza."

Stevie ordered a sundae of hot fudge on pistachio ice cream. With peanut butter sauce. "Oh, and can you put some granola on it, too?"

Carole and Lisa never ceased to be amazed at what Stevie chose to call a treat. They each asked for frozen yogurt.

When the waitress left their table, Lisa continued where Stevie had left off. "Let's pretend I'm not going away at all," she said.

"I'm with Lisa," said Carole. "Let's ignore the obvious and change the subject. So, how did the ride go with Callie? That was so nice of you to look after her and get her to ride her *own* horse."

"No problem," said Lisa, ignoring Carole's

rather pointed comment. "She's awfully nice. We had a good time, except for missing you.

"She was telling us this funny story about one night during her father's election campaign when she had a big research paper due but she had to be at this dinner instead of doing history homework. The paper was about a factory in their state that had been shut down because of toxic dumping. She hadn't had time to do enough research—and then it turns out that at the dinner, she was sitting next to the man who'd been governor when the factory had been closed. He'd signed the papers to do it! Her teacher couldn't believe how much primary source material she'd gotten."

Lisa and Stevie laughed as they retold the story, describing how Callie had written quotes from the former governor on the evening's printed program, on her napkin, even on the palm of her hand, while her father was trying to get votes.

Lisa noticed that Carole wasn't laughing. "Well, I guess you had to be there. Anyway, Callie has done a lot of stuff, and she tells great stories. You're really going to like her when you get to know her better."

"I'm sure you're right," Carole said. Their desserts arrived before she had to say any more.

Callie was glad to have some quiet time with her horse. She'd enjoyed the ride with Lisa and

Stevie. They were nice, and they might even be friends one day. What mattered more than friends, though, was looking after Fez. He was a handful. He was more of a handful that day than he had been when she'd taken him for his test ride. He'd been at Pine Hollow for three days and should have settled in a little bit. As talented as he was, it was going to be a nuisance to have a horse who hated traveling and took a long time to get used to a new stable. Competition horses traveled a lot and stayed in unfamiliar lodgings all the time. She was going to have to find a way around that. Maybe he'd like a stablemate, a dog or a goat perhaps. Maybe she could find some kind of toy for him that he could take wherever he went. Sometimes horses became particularly fond of something in their own stable, a bucket or a hay net. Whatever it was, it would be a sort of security blanket for him. There had to be an answer, because if this was his best behavior, she wasn't going to keep him any longer than the summer lease.

"Whoa there, boy," she said, patting Fez's neck. He liked that and stood still for a moment. He stood still while she picked his hooves, but he got fussy as she was combing him. His ears flicked back and forth and then lay flat against his head. His eyes opened wide.

She put away the comb and took out a brush.

He seemed to like that better. She worked carefully and methodically, trying to see if there were any particular places Fez didn't like to have brushed. He tolerated it.

As she worked, she noticed that there was another girl about her age grooming a horse in the stall across from Fez's. She was wearing a T-shirt that said Pine Hollow. It was the same kind of shirt that Ben had been wearing the day before. In spite of all the talk about how everybody at Pine Hollow took care of their own horses, it seemed that there was at least one stable hand doing an owner's work.

Callie finished using her brush and tossed it into the grooming bucket. It made a louder sound than she'd expected, startling her. Even more, though, it startled Fez. He tossed his head up. His ears went back, and his eyes opened wide until the whites showed. He began prancing nervously, and that was when Callie realized that she might have made a terrible tactical error by failing to cross-tie her horse before she groomed him, though it hadn't seemed necessary as long as he was in his stall.

Callie tried to shift around so that her back was to the door of the stall and not the back wall, where she could be pinned easily, but Fez was blocking her way. He whinnied and fussed. He wasn't threatening her, specifically, but he was upset, and it was a really bad idea to be in a stall with a loose horse that was upset.

Then she remembered the girl across the hall.

"Can you help me?" she asked.

"No, I can't," Emily answered. "Do you want me to call Ben?"

The response stunned Callie. How could anyone refuse to help someone who so obviously needed it?

Then, as suddenly as he'd spooked, Fez calmed down and Callie didn't need help from anyone. She took the set of cross-ties out of her bucket, clipped them onto the walls of his stall and to his halter, and finished grooming him.

"Did you get your horse under control?" the girl across the hallway asked.

"Yes, no thanks to you," Callie shot back.

"But I couldn't—"

"I understand that you *wouldn't*," Callie said, cutting her off angrily. She'd really been in danger. It was inexcusable that someone would refuse to give her a hand. "I don't think I have anything further to say to *you*."

But she had a few things to say to someone else. As soon as she could have an appointment with Max Regnery, he was going to get a piece of her mind about a certain stable hand who was too good to help a rider who was in trouble.

"All right, so there's one thing I have to say about this summer," Lisa began. "And that is that I've heard from Skye. He called me. I can't wait to see him. It's always exciting. He even said there was something he wanted to talk to me about when I get to Los Angeles."

"He wants you to meet his movie star buddies," said Stevie, licking the last bit of fudge off her spoon.

"In which case, I'll give you a list of the ones you *must* give my phone number to," Carole said as she finished her dish of frozen yogurt.

"I don't think so, but count on me to be looking out for your interests if that's what Skye has in mind."

Stevie looked at Carole. "She's never going to come back! She'll go out there, where they have good weather year-round, where she knows the most famous and desirable of all the young stars—"

"Don't be silly," said Lisa. "Not come back? How could you even think that I would ever consider leaving all this behind?" She gestured around her, indicating both TD's and the town of Willow Creek, which lay beyond the windows.

Stevie and Carole glanced around. What they saw was an ice cream parlor that hadn't changed much since the late 1960s. It had probably been humble then, and time hadn't improved it any. Willow Creek was a nice enough town, but there were no movie stars, very few celebrities (unless you counted Mr. Jenson, who had won more than forty-three thousand dollars when he was on vacation in Las Vegas), and zero glamour.

"Look on the bright side," Stevie said. "At least we'll have a good excuse to go to California!"

"Stop it!" Lisa said. "I have no intention of moving out there. I promise you I'll be back in time for school. I'll be ready to come back. The hardest part about this whole summer is going to be leaving. And I don't mean just the saying good-bye part, either. Even getting to the airport is going to be tough. My mother says she can't do it. I think she means she won't because she hates the whole idea. Thankfully, Alex said he'd take me."

"But I've got the car tomorrow," Stevie protested. "I'll need it for work in the evening, and I promised to take Callie over to the tack shop at the mall in the afternoon."

"I know. Relax, Alex told me you'd have the car," Lisa said. "He's going to borrow someone else's. I wasn't expecting you to offer. Besides, Alex really wants to be there."

"I'm sure," said Stevie. "He wants to give you

the kind of send-off that'll guarantee you'll be back."

"Guarantees aren't necessary," Lisa said. "I'll be back. Count on it."

Stevie and Carole were both already doing that.

ELEVEN
11

"Yikes!" Stevie said, looking at her watch and then at Carole. "I promised you a ride home and I still have to shower before I go to work. We'd better get going. Can I give you a lift anywhere, Lisa?" She glanced at the check and put her share of it on the table. Carole followed suit.

"No thanks," Lisa said. "I have to go back to Pine Hollow. I left a library book in my cubby, and I'd better return it today or I might not have a chance." She took out her wallet and added her share.

The three girls stood up.

"We'll talk to you before you go," Stevie said.

Lisa nodded. "Definitely," she agreed. She gave them each a quick hug and headed for the door.

Stevie and Carole walked the short distance to Stevie's house.

"Where's the car?" Carole asked.

"In the garage," Stevie said. Carole was a little

surprised. Normally both Stevie and Alex left the car in the driveway, ready to go in a second. "Wait here, I'll bring it out," Stevie said.

Stevie had backed the car into the garage so that it could be stored with the broken taillight and dented end in the place least likely to be detected by her brother or her parents. She knew she was going to have to confess at some point. She just wasn't at that point yet, and the longer she could put it off, the better. She could tell Carole, of course—but why? If nobody knew, nobody would be nagging her to confess.

In a few minutes Carole was buckled into the passenger seat and the two of them were on their way to her house.

"So, what are we going to do about our farewell for Lisa?" Carole asked.

"We'll go to the airport, of course," Stevie said.

Carole smiled. It was exactly what she had in mind, too. "Alex won't be able to give her all the send-off she deserves," she said. "He's definitely going to need some help from us."

"Definitely. We can do balloons and stuff if you want."

"No, just us," said Carole. "A strong reminder, along with Alex, of everything she's leaving behind."

"That's a deal, and then I can take Callie to the

tack shop on the way back from the airport before I go to work."

"Callie?"

"Well, yes, I promised I'd take her to the tack shop at the mall."

"Aren't you going to a lot of trouble for someone you just met?" Carole asked.

"It's really no trouble. I like driving, remember?"

Carole didn't think driving was the issue. She needed to remind Stevie of the sacrifices they all seemed to be making for Callie Forester. "I was sorry to miss the ride this morning, and I meant to thank you for helping out with Pine Hollow's newest difficult tenant," she said, referring to Callie.

"It was no problem," Stevie said. "I mean, he acted up a few times on the trail, but Callie controlled him just fine. She said she thought it helped having him between Belle and Prancer, too. He'll settle down in a few days, I'm sure."

Carole thought that was probably true; she just wondered when his owner would settle down. For whatever reason, Stevie didn't seem concerned about that. Carole thought it best to drop the subject.

The book was right where Lisa knew it would be. She picked it up, tucked it into her backpack, and was about to leave for the library when she realized she hadn't given Prancer a proper farewell for the summer. She wasn't *just* leaving her human friends for two months.

Prancer's stall was on the far end of the U-shaped hallway that housed all the horse stalls at Pine Hollow. The nice thing about that was that she passed all the horses in the place on her way. She greeted them by name, waving, patting, and talking to them sweetly. Most of the horses were in their stalls. The place was quiet.

"Hi there, PC," she said, giving Emily's curious horse a welcome scratch on his neck. He nuzzled her neck with his damp nose.

"Oh, forget it," she said, giggling at the tickle. "I don't have any goodies with me. Besides, I'm absolutely certain I saw Emily giving you an apple this morning."

He relented and returned his attention to his hay tick.

"Hi, Fez," she said, greeting the horse across the hall. "Are you worn out from our— Oh, Callie, you're in there. I didn't see you."

Callie stood up. "Yeah, I was working on his coat. It's amazing how much mud gets on the coat—to say nothing of his fetlock, which I brushed for five minutes before I got the ball of mud off."

"I know," Lisa said. "Horses are very absorbent. Do you want some help?"

"No thanks. I'm actually finished cleaning up my dirt sponge," Callie said. She brushed her hands off on her apron, stowed the last of her equipment in the bucket, and unlatched Fez's cross-ties. "I really do appreciate your offer of help, though. It seems to me that the riders here are always offering to help out—much better than the staff. And that reminds me that there's something I need to talk to Max about."

"What's that?" Lisa asked. The remark really surprised her. She'd always found everyone at Pine Hollow very helpful. "I mean, what happened?"

"Well, it was partly my fault, I know," Callie began. "I got in here to groom Fez and didn't put him on cross-ties. He got upset and threatening. I asked the stable hand to help me and she refused."

"We don't have any girl stable hands now," Lisa said. "It must have been a rider." She couldn't imagine who would refuse to help.

"Well, she was wearing one of the stable T-shirts," Callie said. "And she was grooming that horse over there—the one you were talking to."

"PC?"

"That's his name?"

134

"Right, this one here," Lisa said. "This is PC, and he belongs to Emily Williams. It must have been Emily— Oh, no. What did she say? I mean, exactly."

Callie described what happened. "I asked her to help me. She said, 'No, I can't,' and then she said she'd call for Ben if I wanted—like I needed help calling for help."

"She was right," said Lisa. "She couldn't help you."

"All I needed was for someone to run over here and hand me the cross-ties. Even a child could do that."

"As long as the child wasn't on crutches," Lisa said.

"What?"

"There's no way you would know, I guess, but Emily has cerebral palsy. She can walk, but only with crutches, and it's slow. When she said she couldn't help you, she meant it. You were going to do a lot better with Ben's help than hers."

Callie put her hand to her mouth. "I didn't know," she said quietly.

"Why would you? Look, don't worry about it. Emily doesn't like special treatment. She always says she's not a disabled person, she's a person with a disability. It's not the first thing she wants anybody to know, and as a result a lot of people

135

get to know her before they notice. That's okay, too."

"As long as they don't insult her the way I did," said Callie. "I . . . I threatened to report her to Max. I thought she was an employee—"

"Well, we're all kind of like employees here, so you weren't so far off the mark on that one."

"Well, I was making noises like I thought she shouldn't be an employee any longer. I must have come off like a total jerk. I'm so embarrassed!"

She stepped out of Fez's stall and closed and latched the door behind her. "Do you think she's still here?" she asked Lisa. "I've got to find her and apologize."

"I didn't see her, but let's look."

The two of them hurried to the office. Denise was behind the desk, trying to straighten out a rider's bill for the month.

"Is Emily still here?" Lisa asked.

"Nope," Denise said. "She left about half an hour ago. She used the phone to call her mother and asked her to come right away. She seemed pretty upset about something. Do you know what it was about?"

"I'm afraid I have an idea," Callie said. "I need to talk to her. Can you give me her phone number?"

"I'm not really supposed to give out phone numbers," said Denise.

"It's important," said Lisa.

The look on Lisa's face must have convinced Denise to get out the stable address book. She jotted down the number and address on a scrap of paper and handed it to Callie.

"Hope it turns out okay," said Denise.

"Me too," said Callie. "Thanks, and bye." She was out of the office before Lisa had a chance to offer to walk with her. Callie wanted to get home and to the phone as quickly as possible.

TWELVE

It was getting harder and harder to pretend that nothing was going to be different that summer. Lisa and Alex had a date—their last date before she left. They'd seen a movie, though Lisa doubted she could have told anyone the name of it or anything about it. She and Alex held hands tightly all the way through the film, and she was far more aware of his presence, the tender pressure on her palm, his gentle caresses on her fingers, than she was of anything happening on the screen in front of her.

He walked her back to her house.

"This is going to be hard," Alex said finally.

"I know," said Lisa. "I guess it's time to acknowledge it, too. We'll talk, we'll send e-mail. You're probably going to be spending more time communicating with me over the summer than you do now."

"Probably," he said. "But it won't be as much

fun." He stopped her in a shadow, and they kissed. "I'll be thinking of you a lot."

"When?" Lisa asked.

"Often," he said, a little surprised by the question.

"Why don't we make a date to think of one another—say every night at nine or something like that?"

"That's midnight here."

"So, you'll still be up. You'll probably be in your room then. You can look out the window at the moon. The very same moon will be looking down on me in California, and I'll be looking up at it at the same time."

"It won't even be dark some nights—"

"So I'll look where the moon probably is," Lisa said. "I'll know. If you're looking at the same time, I'll know. I'll be able to feel it, and that's how I'll know where the moon is."

"How could I have ever been in love with anyone before I met you?" Alex asked. And then he kissed her again.

Lisa took that as a yes.

The house was dark and the phone was ringing when Lisa unlocked the door. Her mother was at what she called Group. It was supposed to be a therapy session, but the group was comprised of women whose husbands had left them. Behind

139

her mother's back, Lisa referred to it as Gripe Therapy.

She picked up the phone in the still-dark kitchen.

"Hi, honey!" a cheerful voice said. It was her father. He knew when Lisa's mother was likely to be out of the house and often called then.

"Hi, Dad," she said, flipping on the light.

"It's just one day now and I can't wait to see you."

"Me too," she said, meaning it. Sad as she was to be leaving Virginia for the summer, she loved her father and was looking forward to having time with him.

"I wanted you to know that I'll be at the airport to meet your plane. Evelyn has all the ingredients to make the vegetarian chili you liked so much, so don't worry about eating any lousy airplane food. We'll feed you when you get here."

"Will Lily still be awake?" she asked.

"Lily is *always* awake," said her father. "Why didn't someone remind me how little sleep babies get at night? The only time she sleeps really well is in the daytime. Whatever it means, it seems to be good for her because she's thriving. Wait until you see her."

"I can't wait. I got the pictures from Evelyn and I can't believe how much she's grown."

"She's a real beauty—almost as lovely as her big sister."

"Thanks, Dad," said Lisa.

"And speaking of her big sister, you got a piece of mail here today."

"What is it?"

"I'm not exactly sure, but it's from WorldWide Studios and the initials on the envelope are *SR*."

"Skye? He said he'd talk to me when I got out there."

"Well, apparently he decided to write first. You can see what he wrote tomorrow."

"As if I could wait that long. Go ahead. Open it and read it."

"Your private mail?"

"What do I have to do to convince the world I'm not in love with Skye and he won't be writing anything all that private?" she asked.

"I guess the best way is to let me read the letter," her father said. She could hear him opening the envelope. There was a pause. "Okay, here it is. 'Dear Lisa, I'm so glad—' yadda-yadda. 'Lots of things to show you—' blah-blah. 'One thing I—' Got it. 'One thing I want to ask you about, though, is if you know anyone who might be interested in working on our show's set this summer. The show is about horses, as you know, and we have a whole stable full of them. One of the assistant stable hands has left and we need to

141

replace her. The job requirements are knowing something about horses and being willing to look after them. It's not glamorous, of course. A lot of it is going to involve mucking out stalls and carrying buckets of water. Do you, by any wild chance, know of anyone, over sixteen years old, who might, possibly, fit that description, who could be persuaded to take a summer job on a television film set?'"

"Wow! Oh, Daddy, can I? Please?"

"You mean you think he might have you in mind for this job?"

"Dad!"

"Well, I guess he probably does," her father conceded. "Sounds perfect. We'll talk with him when you get out here. We have to consider things like hours and transportation, but it might be a good idea."

That sounded enough like a yes that Lisa didn't think she'd have to ask again. Now she really had some news for Carole and Stevie!

"Dad, I'll see you tomorrow. Thanks for calling. Love to Evelyn, and give Lily a little hug, okay?"

"Deal," he said. "I love you, honey."

"I love you, too, Dad."

She hung up the phone just long enough to get a dial tone. Stevie's line was busy. She was probably talking to Phil, and there was no telling how long that would be. Lisa tried Carole next.

Carole was every bit as excited as Lisa about her news. "A whole summer working with horses and Skye Ransom!" Carole said. "Sounds like every girl's dream come true."

"I don't think I'll be spending that much time with Skye," Lisa said sensibly. "He'll be on the set most of the time, or in his trailer, or rehearsing. But I will see him, and, best of all, I'll be with horses. It's almost perfect."

Carole was still grinning when she hung up the phone. That sounded like great news for Lisa. Carole sighed. If only the news around Pine Hollow were better. Lisa would be gone. Stevie wanted to be friends with Callie. And Carole's world felt a little more mixed up than she wanted it to be.

Stevie glared at the phone. It had been glaring back at her ever since she'd walked into the house after work. Its glare was almost as bad as the broken taillight's. She hadn't had any run-ins that night—no crushed impatiens, no mangled garbage cans, and no more dented fenders.

But it was the dented fender that was causing her trouble. Every time she'd looked at her own taillight, she remembered the scratch on the Foresters' car. Her mind was doing flip-flops. One second she was sure she'd done it. The next second it could have been anyone at any time. Then she knew she'd done the damage to her own car that night. How could the Foresters' car not have gotten damaged? But the damage to her car was so obvious—there was no way that bad dent would have made just the tiny scratch she'd seen on the Foresters' car.

She picked up the phone. She had to talk to Callie and Scott—or, worse, their parents. She had to know. No, that wasn't entirely true. She was actually doing pretty well not knowing. Nobody had asked her about it. Nobody had called Pizza Manor and complained. They would have noticed. Wouldn't they?

She hung up the phone. But if she didn't ask, she'd never know. She picked up the phone. In another second she'd cradled it again. Finally she picked it up and dialed. She got a busy signal. That was really good news. She hung up again.

Callie held the phone tightly in her hand and punched in the now-familiar number. This time, she punched in *all* the numbers and listened to the phone ring.

"Hello?" It was an adult, probably Emily's mother.

"Is Emily there, please?" Callie asked.

"Who's calling?"

"This is Callie Forester."

There was a long pause. Emily's mother held her hand over the mouthpiece so that Callie couldn't hear what was being said. Finally the woman came back on.

"Uh, Callie, Emily is busy now and can't come to the phone."

"It'll just take a minute. I promise," said Callie.

"Not now," the woman said.

"May I call later?" asked Callie.

"I don't think she'll be able to talk," the woman said. "Tomorrow, maybe."

"I guess it's getting kind of late," Callie said. "Tell her I'll call again."

"Sure," said Emily's mother. And then she hung up.

Callie couldn't remember a time when she'd done something as thoughtless as what she'd done to Emily, and it bothered her a lot that she wasn't getting a chance to apologize. Not that she really deserved it. She'd been rude. Apologizing wasn't going to change that. It probably wouldn't make Emily feel any better, but it might make Callie feel better. She couldn't wait until the next day. She needed to do something that night.

She turned to her desk and took out a sheet of stationery. If she wasn't able to talk to Emily, she could at least write to her.

145

Everything she wrote felt clumsy and inadequate, but by her fifth sheet of paper, she had something that expressed her shame and sincerity. It would do until they had a chance to talk.

Callie asked her mother if she could "borrow" some of the flowers from their backyard for a friend who wasn't feeling well. It wasn't exactly a lie. Her mother agreed. The impatiens were thriving. She should take some of those. Callie made a pretty arrangement, wrapped the stems in a moist paper towel, and bound it all together with aluminum foil. She put a ribbon around it and clipped her note to the ribbon.

Emily's house wasn't far from hers—perhaps a fifteen-minute walk or five minutes by bicycle. She told her parents she'd be back soon. Her mother said she hoped her friend would feel better. Her father had something else on his mind.

"Callie, can I ask you something?" he said.

"Sure."

"Do you know anything about a scratch on the rear end of the van?"

"Rear?"

"Well, on the side, at the rear. I noticed it this morning. I meant to ask you earlier."

"Um, no, Dad. I don't know anything about that," she said. "I'll see you guys later!" She slipped out the door before her father could ask any more questions. Her father was as persistent as a committee chairman at a televised hearing when he started asking questions. She didn't need that right then. She had problems of her own to deal with without covering for anyone else.

THIRTEEN

Carole didn't work at Pine Hollow on Saturdays—at least she didn't get paid for any work she did at Pine Hollow on Saturdays. That made her all the more eager to be there Saturday mornings because it meant she could do the work she wanted to do: primarily looking after, and riding, her own horse.

This Saturday was going to be a little different. She had to make good on her promise to exercise Fez. Once that was done, she could look after Starlight, and then that afternoon, she and Stevie were going to surprise Lisa by meeting her at the airport. The girls had said good-bye to one another about four times on the phone the night before, amid excited conversations about Lisa's potential job on Skye's show in California. Lisa didn't know she was going to see her friends one more time. This would be a good surprise.

Carole opened the door and checked in at the office. Emily handled the office on Saturday mornings, and she was busily assigning horses for the early-morning class. The plain, battered desk had a small vase of flowers on it.

"What's the occasion?" Carole asked, pointing to the flowers.

"They were a gift," Emily said.

"From an admirer?"

"Hardly. More like an apologizer."

"So? Give," said Carole.

"Kind of strange, but a little nice," Emily said. "It was Callie. Yesterday she asked me for help, which I couldn't give her because running is not my best event, but I did offer to call Ben for her. That ticked her off and she got huffy and threatened to report me to Max or some such. I didn't pay much attention. I guess somebody told her about me and she was embarrassed—embarrassed enough to get my phone number, but when she called, I was getting therapy, and then I went out to the movies with my parents. When we got home, Callie had left these flowers on our doorstep, along with the nicest note."

"Really?"

"Really," said Emily. "Of course, that made me feel bad because I should have explained in the first place."

"You don't have to explain anything," Carole said.

"No, normally I don't. My crutches do it for

149

me. But she couldn't see my crutches. I owed her an explanation. You know I never expect anybody's sympathy—I don't need it—but I do need some understanding, and the only way people can understand is if they have information. Callie didn't have the necessary information. That made her feel like a jerk."

"Is that what she wrote?"

"Just that she felt she'd behaved like a jerk and she hoped I'd give her a second chance."

"And?"

"Well, sure," said Emily. "She tried to do the right thing. And the flowers are pretty."

"I guess," Carole said. "They sure dress up that messy old desk."

"So, are you going to take Starlight out now?"

"No, I'm going to work with Fez first."

"Operation Impress the Congressman's Daughter?"

"No, more like Operation Big Mouth," Carole said.

"Someday soon, you'll find a way to tell Callie that Pine Hollow really doesn't exercise boarders for free."

"If this horse were any fun to ride, I'd keep on doing it forever," said Carole. "But he's not. He's a pain."

"You mean you've finally met a horse you don't like?"

" 'Don't like' may be a little strong. Let me just say that I haven't had much fun riding him. So far we've spent all our time together trying to decide who's in charge. He's winning."

"You'll find a way. You always do," Emily said.

Carole carried that thought to Fez's stall.

Fez was as feisty as ever when Carole passed him on the way to the tack room. Even tacking up this horse was a chore.

"Morning, Ben," she said. Ben was sitting in a corner of the tack room adjusting the leathers on the saddles that the youngest riders would use that morning.

"Morning, Carole," he said. "You working with Starlight?"

"Not yet. Fez comes first," she said. "Can you give me a hand with his tack?"

"Sure," Ben said. He set aside the leathers he'd been working on and helped Carole carry Fez's saddle to his stall. They both knew it wasn't carrying the saddle that Carole needed help with. It was putting the saddle on the irritable horse.

Carole approached Fez cautiously and clipped a lead rope on him for Ben to hold while she put on the saddle. Fez never stopped moving while Carole dodged his prancing.

"This darn horse," she hissed. "He's as bad as his owner!"

151

"She's not so bad," Ben said quietly. "Better than her brother."

That surprised Carole a little.

"What's the matter with her brother?"

"Talks a lot," said Ben.

Carole laughed to herself. Ben wasn't much of a talker. No wonder he resented Scott, who talked as easily as some people breathed. Carole buckled the girth on the saddle and tightened it. Fez didn't play games by holding his breath while she tightened the girth. That was the first really nice thing she could say about the horse.

Ben held Fez's head steady with the lead rope while Carole coaxed him into his bridle, and then he was ready for his ride—with little more than twice the effort any other horse in the stable required for tacking up.

Carole led him out to the indoor ring. She thought it might be wise to work inside where there would be fewer distractions than outside. Also, the younger riders would be using the outdoor schooling ring, and if there was a chance Fez might run away, Carole didn't want it to happen where anyone could be hurt.

Max was there, sitting on a bench, jotting out his lesson plan.

"What're you up to?" he asked. "I thought you'd be riding Starlight now."

"Well, I sort of told Callie I'd give this guy a

workout," Carole said. Fez backed off and tugged at the reins, nearly pulling them out of Carole's hands. She gripped more tightly.

"He's a handful. He'll do well learning a few things from you," said Max.

Carole was flattered that Max thought she could teach this fellow anything, but not at all confident he was right.

"Make sure you touch the good-luck horseshoe before you climb aboard," he said.

Maybe he wasn't so sure Carole could do anything with him. Sighing, she took Fez over to the mounting block, climbed into the saddle, walked him past the horseshoe—which she tagged quickly—and returned to the ring.

Carole began by walking Fez in circles, clockwise and then counterclockwise, to warm him up a bit. He did all right at that, so she asked him to trot. He cantered. She slowed him down to a walk again and began the process over. It was the same thing they'd gone through two days before. She wasn't any more successful, and it wasn't any more fun.

Carole wished Max weren't sitting there. She knew how busy he was, and she hated to disturb him, especially when she was riding so badly. His eyes were mostly on his paperwork, but Carole knew he wasn't missing anything. All his riders were amazed by how many mistakes he could see in a whole classful of riders all at once. The record was eight simultaneous errors, though there were those who suspected that his stream of corrections—"Heels down, hands steady, eyes ahead, legs straight, seat back, shoulders up, chin in—oh, and tuck in your shirttails!"—was more automatic than actual. They were all common errors among new riders, even the shirttails.

The third time Fez bolted to a canter when asked for a trot, Max stopped pretending to work on his lesson plan. He set his papers down and turned his full attention to Carole's struggle with Fez.

Carole tried to ignore Max and to convince the horse to listen to her.

Finally Max interrupted her efforts. "Carole, you're going about this all wrong," he said.

She drew to a halt. "I know, Max. I should keep my hands steady, but he keeps yanking at them. It's almost impossible."

"No, I don't mean that. It's not your form, it's your approach. You're letting him be the boss. From the moment you walked in here with him, it was apparent who was in charge—and it wasn't you."

Carole felt herself flush with anger. She knew better than to express it, though. What she was angry about was simply the truth.

"So?" she said, containing her irritation.

"So, think about it. This is a strong, fiery horse. It's in his nature to challenge authority. If the authority doesn't challenge him back, he's going to assume he's in charge, and, clearly, that's what's happened. You've lost control, and you're never going to get it back."

"Never?" Carole asked weakly.

"Not now, not this way," said Max. "You're being too nice to him."

"I can't hurt a horse, Max!" Carole protested.

"I'm not suggesting that you do," he said. "But I do suggest that you put him away now."

"He needs the exercise," Carole said. "And I don't want to give up on him. I'm better than that."

"Yes, you are," said Max. "So here's what you're going to do. You are going to start all over again, from the very beginning. You have to be in charge, and he has to know it. I don't know why it is that you thought this particular horse wanted a velvet-glove treatment, but you were wrong. He needs a strong hand, a firm voice, a powerful leader. You've been elected. Go do the job." Max sat back down on the bench, crossed his arms in front of him, and waited to see what Carole would do.

Carole had a world of choices in front of her. She could try striking the horse, but she never thought that was the right way. She could try yelling at him. She rejected that because he hadn't shown any indication that he was deaf, so there would be no point. She could yank back at his reins and abuse him in the same way he was trying to get the jump on her, but she didn't like it when he did it to her, so she doubted he'd like it if she returned the favor. Or she could, as Max suggested, start all over again.

She dismounted and led Fez back to his stall. She removed his tack, gave him a quick brushing, some fresh water, and a bite of hay. Then she left him alone.

Ten minutes later she reappeared at his stall, carrying his saddle and his bridle. As she approached the stall, instead of looking fearful—the way she felt—she glared directly into Fez's eyes. He backed up. She wasn't actually threatening him in any way that humans understood. She was merely challenging him in a way horses understood. Fez stood still and glared back.

Without showing any hesitation, Carole clipped a lead rope on him, cross-tied him, and put his saddle back on. She talked to him because it was almost impossible for her not to talk to a horse while she worked on him, but it was in a matter-of-fact tone, not a soothing tone or a fearful one. Her theory was that if she was able to fool him into thinking she wasn't afraid of him and didn't expect him to misbehave, he might not intimidate her and act up.

He stood quite still while she tacked him up. When she took hold of his reins and led him back to the ring, she looked straight ahead. Looking back at him would have appeared questioning. She wasn't in a mood to question anything. She was being positive. He was, for the first time, being relatively obedient. He was still no Starlight or Belle. He wasn't in the least bit docile, but he was obedient. That was all Carole needed from him.

They reached the ring. Carole signaled him to stand still while she mounted, and he did. He tried to take one step while she swung her right leg over his back, and she tugged firmly on the reins. He stopped fiddling.

She walked him over to the good-luck horse- shoe, touched it, and began walking him in cir- cles around the ring. He did what he was told. He shook his head a bit, but he stopped that when she tugged, not yanked, firmly on the reins. She signaled him to trot. He trotted.

He was like a different horse. He had all his power and fire, but he was much more obedient than he had been earlier, at least as well behaved as he had been when Callie rode him.

Max, in his usual reserved manner, just said, "Nice work, Carole."

Half an hour later, still pleased by her success with Fez, she returned the horse to his stall, untacked him, and gave him a quick grooming.

As she worked on him, she wondered at the transformation. It wasn't that this horse hadn't been trained. He had. But she had been allowing him to get away with bad behavior, allowing him to ignore his training. That made it her responsibility to remind him what was okay and what wasn't. She'd done it. She now had a horse that, while not as enjoyable for her to ride as Starlight, was a horse she could manage. Now maybe she wouldn't hate herself so much for the foolish promise she'd made to Callie.

Carole shrugged. If she could transform Fez's personality, maybe she could do the same with Callie. No, that wasn't right. She had to take some responsibility for Fez's problems. She'd let him get away with murder because she'd been treating him like eggshells. She hadn't done that with Callie. Or had she?

She'd definitely gotten off on the wrong foot with Callie, just as she'd gotten off on the wrong hoof with her horse. Maybe she should do something to change that.

Well, if Callie was big enough to make an effort to square her mistake with Emily, Carole thought she should be big enough to square her own mistake with Callie.

In the meantime, she thought she owed Fez a little more reward than she'd given him so far. She decided to turn him out in the paddock. He'd been cooped up in the van and then in his stall long enough. He could use a chance to run free for the afternoon. She got Max's permission to let him stay out until she returned from the airport. Carole walked Fez through the gate, took the lead rope from his halter, and gave him a gentle slap on his flanks to tell him it was okay to run free. He didn't have to be told twice.

Carole glanced at her watch. It was noon. Lisa's plane took off at four. The hard work Carole had done with Fez had used all of her riding time. Now she had to get home, shower, and change her clothes for the trip to the airport.

Her heart ached. Lisa's departure was going to change everything. Just four hours to go.

FOURTEEN

Four hours later, everything in the world had changed.

Stevie listened dully to the rhythmic *slap, slap, slap* of the windshield wipers for a few seconds before she realized what the sound was, where she was, and how she'd gotten there.

"Carole?" she whispered. "Are you okay?"

"I think so. What about you?"

"Me too. Callie? Are you okay?" Stevie asked. There was no answer.

"Callie?" Carole echoed.

The only response was the girl's shallow breathing.

"What happened?" Carole asked, trying to remember the last few minutes. It was all a blur.

"We hit something—a horse, I think. We spun, rolled, and landed. I think we're at the bottom of the hill by Janson's farm across from Pine Hollow."

Carole looked in the backseat. Callie lay still, her eyes closed.

"Callie? Callie? Wake up!" There was no answer. "She's breathing, but she's unconscious," Carole said.

"Can you move all right?" Stevie asked Carole.

"I think so," Carole said. She did a quick inventory. She could feel a throbbing in her wrist, which must have hit the dashboard when they rolled over. She was aware, too, of a dull ache in her arm. She wiggled her toes and her fingers. Everything worked. "Yeah, I'm okay," Carole said. "What about you?"

"I've got an awful ache in my belly where the steering wheel hit me, but everything moves. I'm hurt, but okay."

"Well, we can get out, but we'd better not move Callie. We've got to go for help."

Stevie peered through the windshield, which was still being methodically cleaned by the wipers. She could see lights at the top of the hill.

"No, I think help has come for us," she said.

Carole and Stevie opened their doors. Carole stood up. Rain pelted down on her. In spite of her aches, it made her feel incredibly, wonderfully alive.

She and Stevie looked at the top of the hill, where more flashing lights were gathering. Several people were looking down at them. The girls waved.

"Are you okay?"

"We are, but there's another girl in the car and she's unconscious!" Stevie called back.

"Don't move her!" an emergency medical technician yelled.

Stevie and Carole waited for help to arrive. It didn't take long. Within minutes several EMTs skittered down the hill, carrying a stretcher and medical bags. As soon as they were sure Stevie and Carole could walk, one of them helped the two girls up the hill, while the others turned their attention to Callie.

Carole started to shiver. It seemed strange to be shivering in the warm rain. "It's shock," the ambulance driver said. He gave her a blanket and settled her in the back of the ambulance. He made her lie down and gave her an oxygen mask, though she didn't think she needed it.

As she lay there, Carole began to drift off into a pleasant, painless sleep. Stevie sat beside her, holding her hand.

"Stevie! What happened to Carole? Are you okay?"

It was Max, climbing into the shelter of the ambulance. He'd run all the way from the stable when he heard the sirens.

162

Carole opened her eyes and nodded to Max. "I'm okay," she said. "Just shook up."

"Me too," Stevie said. "But Callie's hurt. She was unconscious in the car. We didn't try to move her."

"Good," Max said. "The EMTs are down there now. But how did it happen?"

Stevie explained. "The rain just came out of nowhere, pelting down so hard I could barely see, and then something came at the car. I tried to get out of the way, but I slammed into it. Was it a horse, Max? Did I hurt a horse?"

"It was," Max said. "The police called Judy. She's with him now."

"Who was it?" Stevie asked, her voice rising hysterically.

Carole didn't need to hear the answer. She knew exactly which horse it was. She knew which horse had been in that paddock, and she knew which horse would be seriously spooked by thunder, which horse had the strength and endurance to jump or smash down one of Pine Hollow's high fences and flee.

"Fez," she said quietly.

"Right," Max confirmed. He put his arm around Stevie comfortingly.

"Is he okay?" Stevie asked.

"He was hurt badly," Max said. "Judy will save him if she can. Look, you two are going to go to the hospital. I'll go back to Pine Hollow and call your parents. They'll meet you over there. I'll come over later. Okay?"

"Okay," Stevie agreed. "Max, I didn't mean to do it. I didn't mean to hit Fez."

"I know that," Max said. "Everybody does. Don't worry about him. Worry about making sure you're all right."

Stevie and Carole nodded glumly. Max left them.

An EMT climbed into the back of the ambulance as a second ambulance drew up behind theirs. The rain that had started so suddenly was tapering off. Through the crowd, Stevie and Carole could see a gurney being rolled up to the other ambulance. Callie was strapped flat onto it. Her eyes were closed, and she had an IV bag suspended above her head. The EMTs who were pushing the gurney looked grim.

"Callie?" Stevie called out. "Is she okay?"

The EMT pulled the doors of the ambulance closed. "They're doing what they can," he said. "Now, let's get you two to the ER."

All her life, Stevie had thought it would be fun to ride in an ambulance, lights flashing, siren wailing. What she'd never fully absorbed before that, however, was that a ride in an ambulance meant something was wrong, really wrong. The thought made her shiver. She pulled a blanket tightly around her.

The siren wailed, the lights flashed. Ahead of them traffic pulled aside to give them the right of way. They drove right up to the hospital door and walked off the ambulance into the emergency room. There were nurses there, offering them wheelchairs, and they were taken to an examining room.

Nobody would tell them anything about Callie.

"It was my fault. I was driving," Stevie said.

"You couldn't help it," Carole consoled her. "You did what you could. The horse ran right at us. I saw it happen."

"There must be something I could have done," Stevie said. She didn't even want to say what was in her heart. Anybody could have an accident. They happened. It wasn't the accident that upset her. It was the consequences of that accident. Callie and Fez, but mostly Callie.

"I never told her I was sorry," Carole said. "I wanted to. I wanted to tell her about how I rode Fez today, but, but . . ." She choked on her own thoughts. Tears streaked down her cheeks.

"Carole! Are you okay?" It was her father. He hurried into the examining area and ran over to her. "And you, Stevie? Are you okay?"

The two girls nodded. "We're both okay,

Dad," Carole said. "I mean, we got some bumps. The EMT thinks Stevie might have broken a rib, but we're basically okay. What about Callie? Did they say anything?"

"Not yet," he said. "They're examining her. She's still unconscious."

Stevie's parents arrived then. Once again she and Carole promised that they were okay. Once again they asked for news of Callie. There was none.

Outside the curtain that surrounded them, they heard the congressman arrive. "Where's my daughter?" he demanded, his voice filled with uncertainty.

"This way, Congressman, Mrs. Forester," a doctor said.

The next few hours were a confusion of questions, X rays, questions, pain pills, and even more questions. Stevie did have a broken rib from the steering wheel. Carole's injuries were limited to scrapes and bruises. Everybody who talked to the girls told them how lucky they were and how smart they were to wear their seat belts. Neither of them felt lucky or smart.

The police asked them questions about what had happened. Stevie and Carole each described the events over and over again. Each time was more painful than the last. Stevie could still hear the awful silence in the car when Callie didn't answer.

Outside, they could see the flurry of activity around the trauma room where the doctors were working on Callie.

Finally, when the doctor said they could go, Stevie stood up weakly and walked over to the plastic-covered couch where Congressman Forester and his wife were sitting with Scott, talking in hushed tones.

"Is Callie going to be okay?" Stevie asked.

"We hope so," said Mrs. Forester. "She's in a coma. The doctors say she hit her head and got a bad concussion. There was some bleeding. They have to operate. They keep saying we're going to have to wait."

Stevie gasped involuntarily. It was so utterly frightening.

"I'm sorry," she said. "I don't know what or how, but if I could have—"

The Foresters just looked at Stevie. The usually garrulous Scott was out of chatter. And so, for once, was Stevie. She didn't know what to say anymore. There were no words to make it better. The best any of the Foresters could do was the nod of acknowledgment that Mrs. Forester gave.

"Come on, Stevie. I think it's time to go home," Mr. Lake said, putting his arm around his daughter. She took strength from his warmth and walked meekly to the car.

It was still raining when they left the hospital. Stevie sat in the backseat of the car, listening to the windshield wipers all the way home.

FIFTEEN

W hat followed were the longest two weeks of Stevie's and Carole's lives. Every time Stevie breathed, moved, spoke, or laughed, her broken rib reminded her of what had happened. Medicine could help with the pain she had in her body, but it couldn't do anything to repair the agony she felt in her heart. Even the comfort of her daily conversations with Carole and Lisa couldn't ease her pangs of guilt.

Fez was getting the best care veterinary medicine could offer. Most horses hurt that badly would have been put down because the cost of healing would be so great and the chances of a successful recovery so slim. The accident had left Fez with cuts and scrapes, which would leave him scarred, and a broken leg, which might have rendered him totally incapacitated. Judy Barker didn't have to spell it out. Everybody knew that a horse bore half its weight on its powerful, muscular rear legs and half its weight on its slim and fragile front legs. Horses asked a particularly heavy task of their forelegs, and weaknesses there were particularly troublesome. The accident had broken Fez's foreleg.

Judy had kept Fez at her clinic so that she could watch him closely. He was suspended in a sling. It wasn't for Fez's leg but for his body, holding him up in a standing position so that his legs just touched the floor. He could reach his grain, water, and hay, but he couldn't walk around at all.

It wasn't easy on Fez. In spite of everything Carole had learned about controlling him, the horse was as enthusiastic about being immobilized in his sling as he had been about being in a van. He flailed and fretted all day long, and every attempt to loose himself from the sling brought a scream of pain caused by his broken leg. Judy gave him as much pain medicine as she dared, hoping to spare him a fate that was worse still.

Stevie and Carole took turns visiting him, anticipating his needs, calming and soothing the fretting horse. By the end of a week, he had learned to trust them just enough that he didn't kick and fuss constantly—merely most of the time.

And while they worked to help Fez, Callie lay in a hospital bed. She had two operations to relieve pressure on her brain, and she remained in a coma. While Stevie and Carole spent every minute they could looking after Fez, neither one of them could stand the idea of seeing Callie. Not yet.

A week after the accident, the police formally dismissed all potential charges against Stevie. Another driver had been on the road, behind Stevie's car. He'd seen everything that happened and said there was no way Stevie could have avoided the horse, which had run straight into her car.

Still it wasn't enough. Even though the law exonerated her, Stevie wasn't ready to exonerate herself.

"It almost doesn't matter what they say," she told Carole. "What matters is Callie."

"At least you were nice to her," said Carole. "I never gave her a chance. I was going to tell her I was sorry, but I couldn't think of a way to say anything when we went to the airport, and now I don't know if I'll ever have a chance."

There was nothing more to say. Fortunately, there was a lot to do. Fez was a demanding patient, and they were determined to do everything they could for him, since they couldn't do anything for his owner.

After two weeks Callie woke up. She opened her eyes for the first time at three o'clock in the morning. Scott was by her bedside, sleeping in a chair, when he heard her speak.

"Hello? Who's there?" she asked.

Scott sat bolt upright, hardly believing what he'd just heard.

"Callie? Are you all right?"

"I guess so," she said. "Where am I? What's going on? What happened?"

Scott was so relieved to hear his sister speak that he almost didn't notice his own tears.

"Oh, it's a long story," he said. "You've been out of it for about two weeks. Do you remember anything?"

"I don't think so," Callie said. "I just remember windshield wipers. I thought they'd never stop. Oh, my god, Stevie and Carole. Are they okay?"

"They're fine," Scott said. "Minor injuries. Now, just relax. I'm going to call Mom and Dad. Then I'll tell you everything. Like I said, it's a long story."

"In that case, get me something to eat before you talk. I'm starving!"

Over the course of the next few hours, Callie learned everything that had happened since the accident. Scott told her how Stevie and Carole were looking after Fez and that they called every day to say how he was doing. Callie's parents came over to the hospital to see her and just hug her. Callie ate some Jell-O, which the hospital provided, and some pizza, which her father brought from home.

And then the doctors arrived. They tested, questioned, poked, prodded, tapped, tickled, and beamed.

"Good . . . Hmmm . . . Interesting . . . Very good . . . Amazing," they said.

In the end they were very pleased with how well Callie was doing.

"When can we bring her home?" her parents asked when they spoke with the doctors in the hall after they'd completed their examination.

The doctors looked at one another. Dr. Amandson shook his head.

"Not for a while," he told them. "You see, she's partially paralyzed on her left side."

"We thought you said she was doing well."

"She is. Extremely well. With the kinds of injuries she sustained, we were expecting much worse. She's doing extraordinarily well, in fact. She is alert. She can talk, think, reason, and use all five senses. The only residual damage to the extreme trauma her brain suffered is that her left side doesn't work very well."

"But paralyzed? What does this mean?" Mrs. Forester asked.

"She's going to need physical therapy—lots of it," said Dr. Amandson. "What's happened, basically, is that some of her brain was damaged—the part that controls movement on the left side of her body. That part of her brain may heal itself in time, or it may not. The brain is a marvelous invention, especially the brain of a young, healthy girl like your daughter. If the damaged part doesn't heal, another part of the brain can be encouraged to learn whatever got lost in the accident. With hard work, concentration, and endurance, Callie will be up and walking soon. Eventually she may be as good as new. The therapist will be here in the morning to help plan a program for her. Now, tell me, do you have any questions?"

"Not right now," said Mr. Forester.

"Yes, one—or maybe a few," said Mrs. Forester.

"Yes?"

"Is Callie out of danger?"

"I don't know," Dr. Amandson told her. "We'll have to watch her closely, for a long time, until we're sure."

"Is there any way this physical therapy could be dangerous to her?"

"No, not really," said the doctor. "As long as it's carefully monitored."

"What kinds of things will they do?"

"The therapist will develop a program that will begin very slowly, building up muscles and working on balance and coordination skills. We've found that the progressive healing of patients in physical therapy is a lot like the way babies learn motor skills, crawling, walking, and so on. They try to create a program that is interesting as well as useful. I don't know Callie other than as a comatose patient. Is there some activity that she enjoys more than others that we might try to incorporate in her therapy? Swimming perhaps?"

"Well, she does like to swim," said Mrs. Forester.

"Horseback riding," Mr. Forester said. "It's the thing she loves the most in the world."

The doctor smiled. "Have you ever heard of therapeutic riding?" he asked.

"No," said Mrs. Forester. "But I have the feeling we're going to hear a lot about it—and soon."

A few weeks after that, Emily found Carole and Stevie in Fez's stall.

"Ouch!" said Carole, shaking her hand. Fez had nipped at her fingers when she gave him a carrot. "Didn't you ever hear the saying Don't bite the hand that feeds you?"

"Being sick has not improved his disposition," Stevie said.

"It rarely does," Emily told them. "And, speaking of being sick, guess who called me. I hate it when people say things like that, so I'll tell you. Callie Forester. She was calling me from the physical therapy room at the hospital. Her therapist thinks horseback riding would be good. They wanted her to go to Free Rein—the therapeutic riding center where I learned to ride—but she said that if she was going to ride again, it was going to be at Pine Hollow. She wants me to be her instructor."

"Perfect," said Carole. "Absolutely perfect. You'll be perfect for her."

"Maybe I will be, but PC definitely will be. He'll be glad to have another rider from time to time." Emily had utter faith in her horse, and everybody who had ever seen him perform knew she had reason to feel that way.

"When will she be at Pine Hollow?" Stevie asked.

"Right, how soon?" Carole echoed.

"We made a date for next Wednesday morning. You'll both be here, won't you?"

"Absolutely," said Stevie.

"Of course," Carole told her. "We wouldn't miss that for anything."

"Good, because she'll be here with her therapist and her parents. I think Scott's coming, too. It's going to be a real family outing for them. There's a lot of work to be done before then, too."

"Yes," Carole said. She knew what Emily meant, but she had work of her own to do before

176

she saw Callie. She had to figure out how to apologize for the past and make the future better.

"Both her parents?" Stevie asked. "They'll be here?"

"That's what she said."

Stevie felt a shiver. The whole family would be there. She hadn't seen them since the hospital. Now she'd see them all. Scott, whom Stevie liked because he was charming and funny, probably wouldn't be funny anymore. Stevie had been driving in the accident that hurt his sister. Congressman and Mrs. Forester wouldn't want to see Stevie because Stevie's car had nearly killed their daughter when it struck their horse.

And Callie?

Could Stevie look at any of them? What would she say? How could she say she was sorry in a way that meant anything when she'd hurt them all so badly? Could she ever face them?

She didn't know.

SIXTEEN

The first person to arrive on Wednesday was
Scott. Carole, Stevie, and Emily were tacking up PC for Callie when Scott came up the
driveway, riding a bicycle.

He looked around uncertainly and then, recognizing Carole, walked over to the girls. Stevie was
glad she was standing on the far side of the horse.
Maybe she'd never have to speak to anyone.

"Hi," Carole said. "I guess it's Callie's big
day."

"I don't know. This seems pretty crazy to me."
Scott shook his head.

"You'll see." Carole introduced him to Emily,
who leaned forward with a crutch under her left
arm to shake hands with her right.

"I know, I know," she said, anticipating his
concern. "You're trying to figure out if this is a
case of the blind leading the blind . . ."

Scott blanched. Clearly Emily had been right
on the mark. "I wasn't going to put it that way,"

he protested, shifting his eyes away from her crutch and back to her face.

"Of course not," said Emily.

"Well, I guess my sister knows what she's doing."

"We'll see, won't we?" Emily asked. "Anyway, I was as uncertain as you are, but I've talked with Callie's therapist, and we have a pretty good program lined up for your sister. Besides, it's not me who is going to be doing the instructing. It's good old PC here. He knows absolutely everything. He's the best teacher in the world." She gave him a firm pat on the neck to punctuate her statement. The well-behaved horse didn't budge.

"You named your horse after a computer?" Scott asked, smiling for the first time.

"No, it stands for Physical Courage," said Emily.

Carole laughed. Stevie smiled tentatively. PC's "real" name was an ongoing joke. Whenever somebody asked Emily what PC stood for, she had a different, and apt, answer.

"Is something wrong with your car?" Carole asked, noticing the bike for the first time. Stevie cringed, shifting herself even farther behind the horse. She had noticed the bicycle immediately and didn't want to hear the answer. It wasn't going to help to talk about cars.

"Uh, no—Well, yes—Sort of," Scott stammered.

It was the accident. Stevie was sure. It had to be. Because of her carelessness, the congressman and his wife must have decided that all young drivers were unsafe. Or maybe it had frightened Scott so much that he couldn't drive anymore.

"I've been grounded," Scott said.

Stevie had to know. "Is it because of me?" she asked.

"No," he said, looking at her for the first time. He seemed to be about to say something but changed his mind. Instead, he turned his attention to Carole and continued. "Not at all. It's because of me. I was driving the Jeep a couple of weeks ago before we moved here and I backed into a stone wall on our neighbor's property. I just made a small dent, but Dad found it last week and blew up at me. It wasn't so much that I'd done the damage, he said, but that I'd tried to hide it. Being a congressman makes him especially touchy on the subject of cover-ups. Anyway, I'm on two-wheel transport for a month."

"S-Scratch? Dent?" Stevie stammered.

"Yeah," said Scott.

"Left rear?" she asked.

"You must have seen it in the body shop, I guess," said Scott. "It really wasn't much of a dent. It won't even reach our deductible, but it definitely annoyed my father. He's tough."

That dent. It seemed like such a small thing compared to everything else that had happened, but it made Stevie feel a little better to know that she hadn't made the dent in the Foresters' Jeep. That didn't change the fact that she'd tried to hide it, but that was too complicated now. She patted PC vigorously to mask her relief.

Carole looked over at Stevie. Stevie never was any good at hiding her feelings. She knew something had just happened to her friend, but she had no idea what. She'd find out later. For now, she had her own weight to lift.

The Foresters' car pulled into Pine Hollow's driveway. Carole could see Callie's parents in the front seat. Callie and another person—presumably her physical therapist—were in the back. It was time for Carole to talk to Callie, to do it right, to start all over again.

She walked over to the car when it stopped and waited for the door to open. With the help of the therapist and a pair of crutches, Callie got out. She was unsteady, unsure, and insecure in every way.

Carole took a deep breath, smiled at the girl, and stepped forward. She was determined to make this a new beginning, just as she'd done that day with Fez when she'd untacked him and started over.

"Callie, I want us to have a fresh start," she said.

Callie nodded.

Carole offered her hand. "Welcome to Pine Hollow," she said. "You're going to love it here, I know."

Callie looked at it uncertainly for a second, then tucked her left crutch firmly under her arm for balance and reached forward with her right hand, much as Emily had done a few minutes earlier with Scott.

"I'm sure it'll be great," said Callie, shaking Carole's hand. She smiled back.

Callie's parents also got out of the car. Max came out of the stable and greeted them warmly. The therapist helped Callie over to where PC was waiting for her. Max introduced Emily and PC to the Forester family.

Callie looked awkwardly at Emily. "I never really—and now—"

"It's okay, Callie," Emily said, cutting off the apology she knew was coming her way. "You already took care of that. What's past is past."

"I only wish . . . ," said Callie. She helped herself forward so that she could pat PC. "This is the boy who's going to teach me to walk again?" she asked.

182

"He's going to do his best," said Emily. "And his best has always been pretty good. Stevie, can you bring him around to the mounting block?"

Stevie had been working so hard to be invisible that she was almost surprised that Emily had noticed her presence. And now everybody looked at her.

She didn't say anything. She just walked the horse to where Callie would be able to mount. As soon as Callie was in the saddle, Emily and the therapist took charge. Stevie, Carole, and the Foresters stood back.

Stevie found herself next to Callie's parents. *Apologize.* She had to do it. She had to say something. She'd been driving. *I'm sorry. So sorry.* The words stuck in her mouth.

She glanced at Congressman Forester next to her. She opened her mouth to speak. And then she closed it. He was watching his daughter on horseback, walking sedately around the schooling ring. Tears filled his eyes. He reached over to Stevie and put his hand on her shoulder as much to silence her as to accept her unspoken apology. He didn't want to talk about it, either.

There would be another time when they could talk, and now Stevie knew that she could say what she had to say—that he would listen and maybe even understand.

The work was done for Stevie and Carole. This

was a time when Max, Emily, the therapist, and the Foresters were all the help Callie needed. Carole and Stevie withdrew and retreated to a shady spot on a hill overlooking the ring where they could watch. It was at times like this that they missed Lisa most. They each wished she could be with them to share their healing, to be a friend. Lisa had a way of seeing the calm center of a confusing world. Her presence touched her friends now from the other side of the country.

"Think she's going to be okay?" Stevie asked, nodding toward Callie.

"Yeah," Carole said. "She'll be fine."

"Not today. I mean ever. Will she get all better?"

"Everything will get all better one day," said Carole. "Probably. You, me, Fez, Callie—we're already better. A little better, anyway."

"I guess," said Stevie. "And I guess we shouldn't ask for more."

"Not yet," said Carole. "There's still a lot of healing to be done. We've got a long way to go."

"But we've started, right?"

"Yes, we've started," Carole agreed.

ABOUT THE AUTHOR

BONNIE BRYANT is the author of nearly a hundred books about horses, including The Saddle Club series, Saddle Club Super Editions, and the Pony Tails series. She has also written novels and movie novelizations under her married name, B. B. Hiller.

Ms. Bryant began writing The Saddle Club in 1986. Although she had done some riding before that, she intensified her studies then and found herself learning right along with her characters Stevie, Carole, and Lisa. She claims that they are all much better riders than she is.

Ms. Bryant was born and raised in New York City. She still lives there, in Greenwich Village, with her two sons.

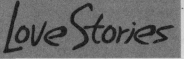